Coon Dogs and Outhouses

Volume 1

Tall Tales

From The Old South

Great Southern Short Stories

Luke Boyd

This Book is Sponsored by TotalRecall Publications, Inc.
1103 Middlecreek
Friendswood, Texas 77546
281-992-3131 281-482-5390 Fax

Printed in United States of America

Printed and bound by Lightning Source, Inc. in the USA and UK

Paper Back
ISBN: 978-1-59095-837-7
UPC 6-43977-5837-1

eBook: Adobe Acrobat
ISBN 978-1-59095-838-4
UPC 6-43977-5838-8

The sponsoring editor is Bruce Moran and the production supervisor is Corby R. Tate.

For Sara

My wife of over fifty-three years,

For her love, help, faith, and encouragement

About the Author

Dr. Lucas G. "Luke" Boyd first saw the light of day in a three-room shotgun house on Jabe Dunaway's place near Anguilla, Mississippi. It was the depths of the Depression. His father had lost everything and had returned to the land to feed his family. However, within a few years he was managing one of those sprawling, 2,000-plus acre cotton plantations the Delta was known for. This plantation culture of his early years left an indelible mark on young Luke.

A stroke of good fortune and a good scholarship allowed him to attend The University of Mississippi, where he earned a B.S. degree. During his career he attended a total of five universities, three of which saw fit to grant him degrees: Middle Tennessee State University (M.S.), The University of Tennessee (Ph.D. in English History). Stints at The University of North Carolina and The University of Chattanooga were for special study in Economics and Far Eastern History, respectively.

He entered the Army through the ROTC program and served for two years as a 1st Lt. in an armored unit.

After leaving the service, he began a career in education which spanned 48 years both at the secondary and college levels. He retired after serving for 19 years as Principal of Battle Ground Academy, a private, college preparatory school in Franklin, Tennessee.

In addition to this volume, his publishing credits include: two books, Coon Dogs and Outhouses, Vol. II, Don't Call Me Hero (ghost writer) the story of a WW II bomber pilot; 9 short stores; 1 article in The Tennessee Encyclopedia of History and Culture. He currently writes regular columns for a local newspaper, The Williamson Herald, and for

Mature Lifestyles magazine.

He and his wife, Sara, have been married for 53 years and have two children and two grandchildren. They live in Franklin, Tennessee.

About the Book

"I never thought it would come to this when I started writing those stories." This is what I said to Sara, my wife, when the offer came to publish a book of them. For me, it was one of those serendipitous events of life which is all the more sweet because it was unplanned and unexpected.

Of course, I have been writing most of my life, but it's mostly been rather formal stuff--pieces that only allowed limited forays down creative paths before reigning the writer in and back to the straight and narrow. This type of writing does have its place and value, if only to teach discipline and to hone skills.

Then, about twenty-five years ago, I realized that my children, especially my daughter, Kimberly, had little knowledge and much less understanding of my growing-up years and the background and culture from which I had come. I decided to try to convey some of this through stories. "The Aviator Cap" was my first effort. Other pieces in this vein were "Ol' Raymond," "The Sanitary Toilet," "The Jesus Doctor," and some of the stories of my father--the grandfather they never knew.

Along the way I began to branch out and to write about other events and incidents--things I thought were odd, amusing, or worth recounting. My father was a good storyteller and I suppose I picked up some of his talents. There is much satisfaction in telling a good story, whether orally or in written form.

I had allowed some of my friends and fellow educators to read some of my stories. They encouraged me to seek publication, but there's a great deal of difference between friends and editors, and my schedule did not allow me to spend time sending manuscripts all over the country. However, in 1995 I saw an invitation by Cool Springs Press to submit pieces for inclusion in its first literary review. To my surprise, the two stories I submitted were both accepted for the first volume of Our Voices.

Through this publication I gained two significant things. The first was encouragement. The second was the opportunity to meet a number of wonderful people--writers, who, even though they toiled in relative obscurity, were passionate about writing and the written word.

When invitations were issued for volume two of Our Voices, I knew the competition would be much keener. So, I submitted three stories hoping to get one accepted. Again, to my surprise, all three made the cut and one was voted the best in the book. Along with this came the offer to do a whole book of my work. It's still hard for me to believe that it has come to this.

In this volume, I've included stories from my early years as well as some I've picked up on my journey. One even came as a dream. I have also taken the opportunity to pay tribute to some people: teachers, friends, and colleagues who have made a difference along the way. We would all be much less were it not for folks like these.

Some of the stories are true, totally; some have been created from and built around one incident. I hope it's hard for the reader to distinguish between the two. Some of the names and places are real; some are not, mainly to protect the innocent as well as the guilty.

All in all I hope I have succeeded in being, according to

my wife's definition, a true Southern writer. Sara maintains that this is someone who can write about nothing and still make it interesting. Some of this may be about nothing, but if it's interesting, I'll count it a success.

Lastly, I want to thank some people whose efforts were instrumental in producing this volume: Sara, who did all the grunt work of typing and getting the material on disk. At times she wanted to censor my language and choice of topics, but showed enormous restraint throughout. I'm also indebted to Steve "Hog Man" Reeves for being in the right place at the right time and to Bruce Moran and all the folks at TotalRecall Publications, Inc. who know how to put it all together.

Table of Contents

Coon Dogs and Outhouses Volume 1

www.totalrecallpress.com

01
Ol' Raymond

He was the first dog I ever knew. The first memories I have of anything or anybody--the house, the yard, my parents--include him. He was as much a part of my family and my early existence as were my parents and younger brother and I loved him greatly.

His name was really just Raymond. I never knew why we tacked the first part on. He surely was not old. I suppose it was a title of affection or endearment.

Ol' Raymond was a red-bone coon hound and a credit to his breed. He was a big dog. I'm sure he seemed big to me because I was so small. But the pictures verify his size. Judging from the size of Gene, my brother, I was somewhere between three and four years old. In one, I am standing at his shoulder and Gene sits astride him like he's riding a horse. The dog and I are about the same height. In another, he carries both of us on his back with ease. As I said, he was a big dog.

He was an outside dog. In that time and place, no one kept a dog in the house. He generally slept on one of the porches in warm weather. In the winter, he would scratch himself out a depression under the house on the south side of the chimney base and use the warm bricks for heat.

Ol' Raymond was a very protective dog. As I roamed about the farm, I knew that I had nothing to fear from anything or anybody as long as he was with me. In fact, he was the protector of the whole family. My daddy was sharecropping a new-ground farm in the western part of the

Delta toward the River. After crops were laid by and during the winter, he was away from home a lot doing carpentry work. We had an unpainted picket fence around the yard and I heard my mama say on more than one occasion, "No, we're not afraid to be here by ourselves. Ol' Raymond won't let anyone inside that fence when Luke's gone." Ironically it was this protectiveness that would prove to be his undoing.

My daddy hunted a lot to put meat on the table. He also ran a trap line trapping mostly mink and raccoon for their pelts. I'm sure the skins didn't bring much by today's standards, but in the mid '30s, any extra income was a bonus. There were usually several skins drying on stretcher boards out by the smokehouse.

He also went coon hunting at night with other men who had coon dogs. They would always come back with coons, but this type hunting was mostly for sport. This was where Ol' Raymond really proved his mettle. Men would come from miles around to run their dogs with him, and I never tired of hearing the stories my daddy told about his prowess in the hunt. My favorite was his confrontation with Pegleg.

Pegleg was a big boar coon who ranged around the nearby bayous. He'd been trailed but never treed, seen but never caught. He got his name because of a missing paw. That leg ended in a stump which left a very distinctive track in the soft, swampy ground. My daddy theorized that the missing paw was chewed off by the coon himself when he got caught in a trap and could free himself no other way. Coons were known to do that.

Anyway, by this time Pegleg was old and grizzled and smart. He knew how to avoid traps and he also knew any number of ways to throw off a pack of dogs who were hot on his trail. Sometimes he would backtrack on his trail and go off in another direction through the trees leaving no scent on the ground. Or he would swim down a creek or crisscross a creek several times to cause the dogs to lose his trail in the water. As a result, Pegleg had never been treed.

One night the men turned the dogs loose and they struck a hot trail immediately. They ran almost in a circle and soon their trailing bark changed to one that told the men that they had their quarry at bay very close by. The hunters hurried toward the sound and came to the bank of a large bayou. The coon's tracks showed the missing paw. It was Pegleg. Only he wasn't up a tree. He was too smart for that. The dogs had apparently picked up his trail very close to him and pushed him so hard that he had no opportunity to use any of his tricks. But the old coon wasn't giving up by any means. The light from the carbide headlamps reflected off his eyes as he sat on a log out in deep water waiting. The other dogs stood on the bank barking. Ol' Raymond was swimming out to get the coon.

Now, the last place a dog wants to confront a coon is in water. A coon will usually wrap himself around the dog's head, forcing it under the water while keeping his own above the surface. In a very few minutes a big coon could drown a dog or whip him so badly that he would leave the fray.

Of course, my daddy had a gun and could have shot the coon, but the dog had brought him to bay and the sporting thing was to allow the dog to try to finish the job even if he got killed in the process.

But Ol' Raymond had fought coons in water before and come out the winner. Instead of trying to hold his head up when the coon climbed aboard, he would do the opposite and push the coon under water, causing him to release his hold to get to the surface. After two or three repetitions of this, Ol' Raymond would get the coon worn down and get his jaws on the coon's neck, ending the fight. But this was not just any coon.

Sure enough, when Ol' Raymond got to the log, Pegleg attacked. He jumped on the dog's head and began biting him about the ears and neck. Ol' Raymond rolled him under and broke the hold. They surfaced and the process was repeated and then repeated again, and again, and again, until my daddy lost count. He confessed that at that point he was wishing he'd shot the coon, but it was too late for that. The two combatants were throwing up so much spray and foam from the murky water and were so closely intertwined that a shot would just as likely hit the dog as the coon. The fight was both furious and long--longer than any fight like this these men had ever seen. Suddenly, the coon let out a squeal that told them that Ol' Raymond had the coon in his jaws and the fight was over. He tried to drag Pegleg to the bank but was so exhausted that the men had to wade out and help him. The men vowed that they had never seen such a fight in all their years of coon hunting and Ol' Raymond's fame spread even farther. The tear in his ear and the cuts on his face and head would heal and be worn as proudly as a dueling scar--the marks of a coon dog who had fought and won.

It Happened on a Saturday

I know it was a Saturday because we had been to town. We never went to town any other day because there was too much work to do to waste time going to town during the week. My daddy would usually work until noon on Saturday. After we ate, Mama would get the number three washtubs down from their nails and fix bath water for all of us and we'd get our only full bath of the week. Then, we would all pile into our Model T Ford and head for the bright lights of Rolling Fork, a town with a population of about eight hundred. My parents would purchase whatever staples we needed at the grocery store where, if I were good, I'd get to have a cold Orange Crush from the ice-water filled drink box. Most of the rest of the time would be spent sitting in the car watching people pass by on the town's main street. We couldn't stay late since we had to get home to do the milking and other chores before dark.

On this particular Saturday when the Model T rolled to a noisy stop beside the house, something was amiss. Ol' Raymond did not come to the side gate to greet us. "Where's Ol' Raymond?" I asked.

"He's probably run off chasing a rabbit or squirrel," Mama responded.

"Naw," my daddy replied, "he wouldn't leave the house with no one here." As he got out of the car, he added, "There he is lying up there on the porch."

"Is he just asleep and didn't hear the car?"

"He had to hear the car. He's laying funny."

"Do you reckon he's sick? Do you think something's

wrong with him?"

"I don't know. Let me go see," said Daddy as he moved toward the house.

We stood by the car and watched him walk up on the porch and squat beside the dog. He felt around on him, moved his legs, and examined him carefully around his head. The dog hadn't moved. Daddy stood up and came slowly back to the car. He had a look on his face I'd never seen before. "He's dead. Somebody poisoned him."

Mama began to cry. Gene was too young to understand what had happened. I didn't really understand either. I had heard about death, but I really didn't comprehend what it meant. In my short life, no person or animal I had any connection to had died. I just knew that the feeling I was feeling inside was not good.

Daddy went back up on the porch, gently picked Ol' Raymond up in his arms and carried him around to the back of the house. When he came back, we were still standing by the car. "The chores have to be done," he said.

Mama went to milk and Daddy went to tend the livestock. Gene and I sat on the front porch. I kept wanting to see Ol' Raymond come bounding around the house and up on the porch to greet me as he always did with his tail wagging as he administered wet licks to my face and hands. But it didn't happen. I thought if I closed my eyes and wished hard enough, Ol' Raymond would come. I tried. I tried real hard, but the only thing that came was the darkness.

Why would somebody poison a person's dog? I've thought of that often since that day. Mama said it was just pure meanness. Daddy said that some people are always wanting to steal something and they just don't like good watchdogs in general and they try to get rid of as many of them as they can. We surely didn't have anything worth stealing. The most valuable thing we had was the meat in the smokehouse. Whoever did it knew we weren't home, so he just walked by, threw a piece of poison-laced meat into the yard, and kept on going. When Ol' Raymond knew something was wrong, he came to the front door for help, but there was nobody there to help him. Some lowdown human had done what the toughest coon in the swamp couldn't do.

After supper Daddy got up from the table and said, "We'll have to bury him." He got a lantern and lit it and we all followed him out back. He stopped at the tool shed for a shovel and continued down the path that led to the field. When he located a suitable place near the corner of the backyard fence, he sat the lantern down and began to dig. The black buck-shot soil offered little resistance to the shovel and Daddy soon had the grave dug. Then, we all went up to one of the outbuildings where Daddy had put him. On the way back, Mama led the way with the lantern; Daddy came next carrying Ol' Raymond; Gene and I stumbled along behind.

As Daddy was about to lay Ol' Raymond's stiffening body in the grave, Mama said, "Luke, we just can't put him in the cold ground. Let me go get something." She took the lantern and hurried back to the house returning shortly with an armload of newspapers. She got down on her knees and lined the grave with them. Daddy put him in and we all said goodbye. Mama covered him up with newspapers, tucking them in good so the dirt wouldn't get on him. Then, we stood and watched as Daddy shoveled in the dirt.

As I stood there, I had a hurt somewhere down deep inside me that made me hurt all over. And the tears rolling down my cheeks didn't help any. And that hurting stayed with me for a long time. I've experienced the deaths of my parents, grandparents, and numerous friends, but I don't think my feeling of grief has ever been any greater than it was the night we put Ol' Raymond in the ground.

Even as this was happening, I could not accept the fact that Ol' Raymond was gone for good. I had seen Daddy plant things in the garden and corn and cotton in the big fields. Not long after the planting, green shoots would be pushing up through the ground. Why would this not be the same?

As Daddy was rounding off the dirt on the grave, I asked, "Daddy, will Ol' Raymond come up?"

He stopped and leaned on the shovel for a few seconds before he answered, "No, son, he won't." But I persisted, "Daddy, I think he'll come up."

"No, son, I'm sure he won't."

But I would not accept that answer. I was sure Ol' Raymond was going to come up out of that ground just like a stalk of corn did. For a long time, I went to his grave everyday and looked for a paw or his nose. No matter what anyone said, I just knew it would happen. In fact, I can remember two or three times going to my mother and saying, "I just passed Ol' Raymond's grave and I saw his nose sticking out. He's coming up, Mama." But each time I was told that it was just my imagination which, indeed, it was. Eventually, I had to accept as true what my parents were telling me. Death was final. I would never see him again.

Ol' Raymond deserved better. He was a credit to his breed. He was faithful and brave. He helped his master in the hunt and he protected his family when he was gone. He didn't deserve to be done in by a coward with some poison in a hunk of hog meat. It would have been better for him to have been bested by some tough old boar coon out in a bayou amongst the cypress knees and water snakes. That would have been a noble end for a noble dog.

02
Daddy's Stories

Introduction

My father loved to tell stories and tall tales. Some were true. Others had some elements of truth in them--maybe just enough to make the listener think they could be true, at least until toward the end of the tale. He had a way of making an observation or turning a phrase that would catch your attention and make it easy to remember. I recall one such phase at one of our Fourth of July fish fries.

Our little country community where I spent my junior high and high school years got together every year for a big fish fry on July 4. There weren't any public parks close enough to go to. Someone would scout around and find a place on the bank of the river or the shore of a nearby lake. Some would come early in the morning, eight or nine o'clock, bringing pickup loads of rough lumber. They would set to building a long serving table and benches all out among the trees. The fire pit would be dug and firewood gathered. A support for the big black wash pot in which catfish and hush puppies would be fried would be constructed. Later in the morning others would come bringing all sorts of vegetable dishes, salads, and desserts to round out the meal.

We were usually the only ones around, but this particular year we had selected the shore of a horseshoe lake near the Tallahatchie River, and another group had come in about fifty yards up the shoreline. Only they were not having a fish fry. The first thing they set up was a very large, black pot. I'd never seen one so big. It must have been five feet across and was so heavy it took several men to get it into position. They filled it about half full of water and started a big fire under it. Then, they began to put all manner of things in the pot. It seemed like everybody added something different. There were whole onions, potatoes, tomatoes, okra, and a number of vegetables we could not identify. The meats were equally varied. We could agree that there were pieces of pork and beef, whole squirrels, rabbits, and quail, and several other things we couldn't name. I had been sitting around with a group of the men who were watching this operation and making comments about this communal stew being created before our very eyes. A late arrival joined our group and observed the activity for a few minutes before asking, "What in the world have they got in that pot?" My daddy replied, "Well, D. J., the best I can figure out, they've got everything in there from bull nuts to cooter." (Cooter was a local term for a turtle.)

Since these are my daddy's stories, I'm going to try to write 'em like he told 'em.

The Kicking Gun

One day early last fall, before the cotton was ready to pick, a bunch of us were down at the store sittin' around on the porch visitin' when ol' Bill Butler drove up. The conversation got around to guns and huntin'. Bill told us about what happened to him a coupla weeks before.

Said he had gone to town to get a piece for one of his wagons and had stopped by the feed store. There were eight or ten fellows, some he knew and some he didn't, sittin' under the shed. They were talkin' and swappin' knives when one fellow Bill didn't know started tellin' them about a shotgun he had. Said it was the hardest kickin' gun he'd ever shot. Some got to askin' about it, so he went and got it out of his truck.

Everybody looked at it. It was a Remington pump and it wasn't very old. Said he wouldn't mind tradin' it off. At that, Bill went out to his truck and got his gun and let the fellow look at it. Bill's was a pump, but it was an older model Stevens. The Remington was much better and newer, but Bill could really shoot his old Stevens and wasn't too hot to trade. At least that's what he kept saying. But that fellow was in a tradin' mood, so he offered to throw in an almost new Barlow knife to boot. Bill thought he had himself a mighty good deal, so he agreed and they swapped right there.

Now, the fellow had warned Bill that the gun would kick, but Bill said he'd been shootin' all kinds of guns for thirty years and figured there wasn't a gun around that could get the best of him. Well, he was wrong. Said he'd been out with it three or four times and the gun had about kicked him to death no matter what he did. Said the last time out he'd missed several easy shots because he was gettin' afraid of how hard the gun was gonna kick him.

At that point I started kiddin' him about not bein' much of a man and not knowin' how to shoot, to let a little ol' gun get the best of him. Well, that kinda got away with him and he said, "All right, Luke, you think you're such a hotshot shooter, you just take this gun out and see if I'm not tellin' the truth. I'll even give you a handful of shells so you won't have to use up any of yours." With that, he went to his truck, got the gun and put in my truck. I didn't have much choice but to take it huntin', but I figured I could shoot most anything made.

Squirrel season hadn't been open long, and I'd planned on going the next morning anyway, so I figured I'd just try out Bill's new Remington. It was a nice gun . . . had good balance. It couldn't be that bad.

I got into the woods about daylight. The leaves were dry, which made it hard to move quietly. I was creepm' along when I heard a squirrel jump. I figured he'd heard me and was on the run. I saw him run down a limb in a tree to my left and jump to a farther tree. I saw the end of the branch he was goin' to land on, so I snapped the gun up with a bead on that spot and pulled the trigger when he landed on it.

I'd had to shoot so fast that I wasn't set good and was a little off balance, too. Well, I want to tell you, I've had mules kick me that didn't kick that hard. That gun kicked me back over a log and into a bunch of scrubby bushes. It stunned me for a coupla minutes. When I came to my senses, I blinked my eyes to clear my head and tried to figure out where I was. My feet were up on the top of the log and I was layin' on my back in amongst those little bushes.

Just as I started to swing my feet off the log and get up, I heard it. There was a rustlin' in the leaves off to my right. I froze. This was rattlesnake country, and it sounded just like a big rattler. My position was pretty awkward and I knew it'd take me several seconds to get untangled, so I thought I'd better see what I was goin' to have to deal with. If it were a rattler, he might be movin' away. But he wasn't. The sound was comin' closer. He would move a little, stop, and then move again. I held my head as still as I could and cut my eyes as hard as I could to see what it was. At first, all I could see was the leaves and bushes movin', but then I saw it.

At about that point, one of his listeners would not be able to contain himself any longer and would blurt out, "Was it a rattlesnake? ! "

Daddy would pause for effect, look all around his audience, and reply, "Naw, it was that gun backin' up to kick me again."

Deer Camp

A long time ago when I was younger, I used to go to deer camp two or three times a season. Back then a lot of the Delta had not been logged, so there was a lot of the big woods left and a lot of deer in them. There were several camps around. I liked to go to one down in Sharkey County.

The folks who ran them would usually set up about the same place every year. They had to be close to a spring or a good source for water. Some of them would drive down a pipe and make an artesian well. The underbrush would be cleared and tents set up. Each tent might have five or six hunters dependin' on how many canvas army cots would fit in. There would be one large tent with rough tables for cookin' and eatin'.

Hunters would pay so much per day or week with most staying a week at a time. The camp provided a cook, food, dogs, and dog handlers. Hunters just had to have their huntin' clothes, guns, and shells.

One year me and a friend of mine, Ozzie Williams, went together to this one I was tellin' you about. It was way back in the woods. They picked you up at the end of the road and took you the last two or three miles by wagon.

There wasn't much to do after supper except to play poker or drink or both. One night toward the middle of the week, Ozzie and I were sittin' around havin' a drink or two. We were sorta feelin' sorry for ourselves because neither one of us had killed a deer yet. I suppose that caused us to have one or two too many and led us to doin' what we did. I don't think we'd 'a done it otherwise.

The cook was a little ole gnarled up man we all just called "Cookie." His real name was James or somethin' like that, but nobody ever used it. A lot of the hunters gave him a rough time about the food and teased him about most anything. With the kind of food he had to start out with and the cookin' facilities he had, there was no way he was goin' to cook up anything real good. But I thought he did a pretty good job.

Well, Cookie's big aim was to kill him a deer and he worked at it real hard. Everyday after he'd cleaned up after breakfast and before he had to start supper, he'd walk out to a stand he had pretty close to camp and wait for a deer to come by. He'd been at this for four or five years and hadn't even seen a deer. But his lack of success had not reduced his enthusiasm. If anything, he'd gotten more determined with the passage of time.

Cookie's gun was an old, and I do mean old, muzzle loadin' musket with a bell-shaped barrel. It was the only one I ever recall seein' outside a museum. Of course, he got teased about it a lot, but he was not fazed by all the jokes at his expense. Much of his conversation around the cook tent was about what he was goin' to do when that big buck came into range.

Well, on the night I was tellin' you about, Ozzie and I got to talkin' about Cookie's musket. We decided that if he were going to kill a buck with it, he'd need a big charge of powder. So, we went over to the cook tent where he kept it and fixed it up. We pulled the ball and charge he had in it and put in a whole bunch of powder and tamped it in with some waddin'. Next, we figured that much powder needed more than one ball, so we just put in a double handful. By the time we got the last waddin' tamped in, the barrel was about full. I guess we thought he'd just find that barrel full of powder and shot and take it out. Even if he didn't find it for a day or two, we didn't think he'd have any reason to fire it, since he never saw a deer anyway.

The next morning after breakfast, the dog handlers loaded the dogs up in a wagon and headed out. Some other camp folk took us to our stands. Ozzie and I were pretty close together that day. We all had to be in place before daylight 'cause that's when the handlers would turn the dogs loose. They would get the deer stirred up and movin' around, and if they stayed on any of the trails they'd been usin', they had to go by somebody's stand.

About an hour after daylight, I heard the dogs. From the sound, they must have been pretty close on some deer's trail. The sound changed directions two or three times and then swung over in the direction of the camp. Before long, there came the most gosh-awful explosion I'd ever heard. It sounded like somebody had fired a cannon. Cookie had shot off that musket with that charge of powder and ball!

I set off to runnin' through the woods toward camp. Pretty soon I spied Ozzie doin' the same. We knew Cookie had to be dead. That old musket surely exploded and probably blew Cookie into several pieces. I could see me and Ozzie in jail for the rest of our lives. From the look on Ozzie's face, I could tell he was thinkin' the same thing.

When we got close to camp, a lot of shoutin' and other commotion led us to Cookie's stand. We both pulled up in amazement. First of all, Cookie wasn't dead. Those dogs must have run a whole herd of deer past Cookie's stand and he had fired into them. That old musket had to have been made out of some heavy, strong metal. It hadn't exploded, but it did have a split barrel. Those musket balls must have gone through those deer like a load of grape-shot out of a cannon. Two deer were dead on the ground and two more had been broken down in their hindquarters so they couldn't run. Blood on the trail indicated that several more had been wounded.

Although Cookie was alive, he was not without injury. The musket had kicked back so hard that it dislocated his shoulder and knocked his arm out of its socket, so that it was hangin' almost down to the ground. He had the musket in his left hand and was goin' along beside one of the wounded deer which was trying to crawl away, and he was hittin' the deer over the head with it. When Cookie saw us, he yelled, "Y'all come help me! If I'd 'a had another half a charge, I'd 'a got 'em all!"

The Stone Mountain Deer

I want to tell y'all about a place I went to over in Georgia years ago. They call it Stone Mountain. It's a big mountain made entirely of granite, and it's completely round. I've never seen anything like it before or since. It's a sight to look at.

Now, as amazin' as that mountain was, there was somethin' just as amazin' that lived on it. A big buck deer with the biggest rack on his head that anybody had ever seen. Those that had seen it said it was as big as a rockin' chair.

I asked some of the local folks why nobody hadn't shot that buck and put that trophy on their wall. They said that many had tried, but none had been successful. They said they had decided that it was impossible to shoot that buck because he was too fast. He had a trail about halfway up that mountain that he ran round on. When somebody came to hunt him, he would start runnin' around the mountain so fast that it took two people to see him. One had to say, "Here he comes." And the other had to say, "There he goes." They had tried every way in the world to shoot him, but none worked. If you tried to shoot straight at the mountain, he'd be gone before you could pull the trigger. Some had thought they could line up with the trail and shoot at him as he ran by. They tried that, but he would outrun the bullet and go on around the mountain while the bullet went straight on out into space. There just wasn't any way to kill that deer.

Well, y'all know how I love to hunt deer, and I've killed my share. I just knew there had to be some way to get that buck. So I had them take me out there so I could see for myself. Everything they said was true. That deer was so fast that when he started runmn' around that mountain, you couldn't even see him the first few times around. You knew he was comin' by 'cause you could hear the clippity clop of his hooves on that granite. After a few trips, you could see somethin' go by, but you couldn't make out that it was a deer. It was just sort of a brown flash as he went by.

I walked around and studied the situation for a while, and decided that the only chance you'd have of hittin' that buck would be to get the bullet to follow the same trajectory as the deer. Since the mountain was completely round, I measured the degree of its curve. Then, I took my rifle to a gunsmith and had him bend the barrel that many degrees to the left, since that buck always ran in a counterclockwise direction.

It took me a coupla days to get this done. By this time a whole bunch of people had heard about what I was doin', so they all came out to see how my plan would work. I got my gun all set up. I wedged the barrel in a tree fork and scotched it steady once I got it in line with the curve of the mountain. I was ready. Before long, that buck came by. As one hollered, "Here he comes," I started to pull the trigger. The gun fired just as the other fellow yelled, "There he goes." And in an instant, both deer and bullet were gone around the mountain.

In a few minutes we heard the deer come by again, but we didn't hear just the sound of his hooves on the granite. What we heard was: "Clippity clop, Zing."

The "Zing" was the bullet following the deer. This went on for several trips.

"Clippity clop, Zing."

"Chppity clop, Zing."

"Clippity clop, Zing."

Before long, he began to slow down so we could see the flash as he went by. We could still hear the "Zing," so we knew the bullet was still after him.

After a little while, he'd slowed down so that you could barely make him out and the "Zing" was still there.

Finally, he slowed down so that you could really see him. He was a fine specimen of a deer. He was stretched out with his head back and that big rack sort of layin' on his shoulders. And then, I saw the bullet. It was about ten feet behind him and it was workin' so hard to keep up, until drops of sweat as big as the end of your finger were fallin' off it.

03
After Bedtime Stories

My father was a great talker and storyteller. I suppose he acquired a good bit of this skill during the time he was a traveling salesman. He had several tall tales that he told on a regular basis, but what I liked best were the stories that were swapped when my uncles came to visit. There were thirteen children in Daddy's family, ten boys and three girls, which meant that there was as much as ten to fifteen years' difference in some of their ages. Even though they all had grown up in the same house with many of the same neighbors, the age differences gave them all different stories, and most of them were as good as Daddy in telling them.

None of my relatives lived close by, so when they came, they usually stayed several days. This was in the early 1940s, but their stories were about people and events at the turn of the century a time that seemed far in the past then and seems even farther today.

The story sessions usually occurred after supper. The children could listen in, but we could not participate in any way or interrupt with questions. Those who could not follow these ground rules were invited to go elsewhere. I always stayed.

Because "you children need your sleep/' we were usually sent to bed at about 9 o'clock. The grownups would stay up and talk sometimes way into the night. It always seemed to me the best stories were told after we were in bed and supposedly asleep. Of course, we were just in the next room and the door was open, so we could hear everything if we could stay awake. My brother usually went to sleep before his head hit the pillow, but I would fight to stay awake to hear what was being said. I would pinch myself, sit up in bed, and do all sorts of things to keep from dozing off.

It was not unusual for two of Daddy's brothers to be visiting at the same time. These were always the best sessions. Everybody would be adding to the stories or asking questions about a specific point until it was almost impossible at times to tell who the main storyteller was. The following stories came from those sessions.

Papa was a nightrider

On one occasion we were sent to bed at the usual time, and for some reason, I let myself fall asleep. I don't know how many tales I slept through before I awakened with a start to hear one of my uncles say, "Do you really think he was one of 'em?"

"Well, I've heard tell that he was."

"I've more than heard. I know he was."

"Aw come on. You don't know Papa was a nightrider."

"I do, too, know he was. If you'd seen what I saw one night, you'd know it too."

"Well, how come me or Vasco didn't see it?"

"'Cause you two had already left home and I wasn't about to tell anybody about it. Nobody was supposed to know who they were and I wasn't about to talk about it and have them pay me a visit even if Papa was one of 'em."

"Well, what did you see?"

"It was late one night. I don't know how late but the horses woke me up. I went to the window to see what was going on. What I saw when I looked out almost made me pee in the floor. There were about eight nightriders on horses. All of 'em had on robes and hoods so you couldn't tell who they were. Two of 'em had pine torches. I thought they were paying us a visit, but I couldn't imagine why. Just then I noticed Papa's horse tied to the post out front and someone came from around the house, untied him, and mounted him. He had on a robe and hood like the rest, but he had on Papa's boots and he got on Papa's horse. It had to be Papa. The whole bunch rode off down the road."

"Well, I guess Papa was one."

"They did some good, you know."

"Sure they did. If you wasn't doing right, you didn't need but about one visit from the nightriders to get you to make some changes."

"I heard tell that they got aholt of ole Charlie Beard one night."

"What did he do?"

"Well, you know he was bad to drink and beat his wife and kids when he got home. One night he was in the middle of beatin' on 'em when the nightriders showed up. Cured him right straight. He stopped hurtin' his family and quit drinkin', too. Started going to church. In fact, he got to goin' to church so strong some of the folks wanted to make him a deacon."

"Did you ever see 'em again?"

"No, and I never wanted to. From then on, if I heard horses in the night, I just pulled the covers up over my head and stuck my fingers in my ears till they went away."

"Well, ain't that somethin'. Papa was a nightrider."

After hearing that story, I had a different perspective of my grandfather. I only thought of him as a fat old man sitting in his favorite chair dozing most of the time. But in his younger days he had been a vigilante riding through the night making sure that the people along the Bogue Chitto behaved themselves.

That Caldwell Girl

"Say, whatever happened to that Caldwell girl?"

"Which one?"

"You know, the one that was so good looking. I think her first name was Burney, or somethin' like that."

"Oh, I know the one you mean. Her name was Brunie. Brunie Mae."

"Yeah, that was it. She was younger than me, but we were always talkin' about how pretty she was. I'll bet she got her pick of the men when she got grown."

"Well, she did for a while, but things changed after the accident and she never got married. She's an old maid."

"You don't mean to tell me Brunie Mae Caldwell's an old maid? It must have been some kind of serious accident to cause that."

"Well, it wasn't exactly the accident. It was more the story about the accident that done it. It was about the thunder mug."

[Note: For the uninformed, a thunder mug is a large ceramic chamber pot. It probably got this nickname from its tendency to act as an echo chamber and amplify the sound that occurred while it was being used.]

"The thunder mug! Aw, come on. You've got to be pullin' my leg on this 'un.

"Naw I'm not. I'll tell you what happened. One night Brunie Mae got up out of bed to use the thunder mug. The thing musta' been cracked or somethin', 'cause when she sat on it, it broke. Busted all over the place, I was told. Now, that should have been the end of it, but one of her brothers told one of his friends, and this friend told somebody else and so on. You know how somethin' like that goes. Well, somewhere along the line, somethin' got added to the story and the story that came out of all this was that when the thunder mug busted, Brunie Mae was cut very seriously in a very strategic place. In fact, this cut was so serious that it rendered her unfit for marriage."

"That's amazin'. Did it really?"

"Naw, I don't think she got cut at all, but once that story got out, nobody could get it stopped. Her brother tried to tell people it wasn't so, but folks accused him of lyin' for her. And you know she wasn't goin' to let anyone examine her. The boys quit comin' around — even the ones who wanted to. They couldn't stand being kidded about courtin' 'damaged goods.'"

"That's really somethin'. Brunie Mae Caldwell, the prettiest girl along the Bogue Chitto. Turned into an old maid by a busted thunder mug. I swanee. I swanee."

Old Seth Jackson

"You know, I've heard that you and those other boys really treated old Seth Jackson bad there one time."

"What other boys you mean?"

"Well, I hear tell they were mostly some of our Beard and Dunaway cousins. Y'all used to get together and ramble around the community playin' pranks on folks."

"We did. We did. But we never did any real harm and that thing with Seth was us just sort of leadin' him to do what he wanted to do in the first place."

"What do you mean by that?"

"Well, I'll tell you just what happened. You know that Seth's place was right next to Jacob Proctor's. Jacob was a real good farmer and Seth wasn't. Jacob's crops were always about the best around. Everything he planted grew and produced. On the other hand, it seemed like when Seth planted cotton he got more weeds than anything else.

"The main crops were bad enough, but what really got Seth's goat was the watermelons. Jacob always had about an acre patch and they were always big and sweet. He even won some ribbons with them at the county fair several times. People were always complimentin' his melons and takin' on about 'em and this really made Seth jealous. Seth's melons were all right, but they couldn't hold a candle to Jacob's. Seth got more jealous every year until he came just about to hate Jacob. We all knew about his feelins' and that set the stage for us.

"Seth liked moonshine pretty well. So, one night we bought a jug from ole one-eye Pete and went by Seth's place.

We gave him a swig or two and told him we were going to ramble around some and that he could come along if he wanted and share the jug. He did and we struck out. We'd stop ever so often to pass the jug. In the dark, Seth couldn't see that we were just holdin' it up to our mouths and not drinkin'. After he got pretty drunk, we started talkin' about Jacob Proctor and that really set him off. He cussed Jacob and really got to carryin' on about him. Then one of us mentioned the watermelons and that was like tyin' a lighted corn shuck to a cat's tail. 'Course we egged him on a little every now and then. He finally said that what Jacob Proctor deserved was to have all his melons busted and the vines pulled and stacked around a stump. Being the good drinkin' buddies we were, we offered to help him do it."

"Seth was pretty drunk and disoriented by the time we got to the watermelon patch. That patch really looked pretty in the moonlight and I said it would surely be a shame to tear up such a nice melon patch. But Seth wasn't about to back down. He said he'd come to tear up Jacob's patch and he meant to do it, and if we wouldn't help, he'd do it by himself. So he started in to bustin' melons and pullin' up vines. After he had a good start, we helped him finish the job. It was a big patch and it took a good while to do it with all of us workin' pretty steady at it. Even in the moonlight where you couldn't see real good, that patch really looked bad with busted melons all over the place and that big pile of vines stacked up around that stump.

"All that exertion and moonshine had taken its toll on Seth and we had just about to carry him home. Jenny was awful mad when we got there, so we didn't stay longer than it took to lay him on one of the beds."

"And he had no idea what he'd done?"

"Naw, he didn't that night. But when he started out to the barn the next mornin' and saw all his melons busted and the vines stacked around the stump, he knew we'd led him to his patch rather than Jacob's."

"What'd he do?"

"What could he do? He couldn't get us for messin' up his patch 'cause he'd helped do it. And he couldn't tell anybody that it was a mistake, that it was supposed to have been Jacob's patch that got messed up. We had him by the short hair with a down-hill pull and he knew it. He did get a lot of sympathy from folks in the community which made him feel good — or at least better. Jacob even came over and told him to pick melons from his patch 'cause he had so many that year."

"Did he?"

"Yep, he did. Ol' Seth swallowed his pride and picked melons from the patch he intended to destroy. You know, he wouldn't speak to any of us for about six months, but I think we taught him a good lesson that night. Yep, I think we did."

Lillie Jean Buckner

"Y'all remember Lillie Jean Buckner?"

"Sure do. Sure do. She was the scandal of the community there for a while."

"What ever did she do with that baby that was born on the other side of the blanket? I think it was a boy, wasn't it?"

"Yep, I think it was. Well, they just raised him as one of her little brothers and he probably never knew the difference. They had a whole bunch of kids which Miz Buckner produced on a regular basis. And she was so fat no one could tell if she were pregnant or not. Ever so often another youngun' just sort of appeared. They didn't have no place to send Lillie Jean off to, so when she started to show, they laid her in and wouldn't let her go out or no one see her and one day there was another little Buckner at the house."

"But everybody really knew?"

"Sure they did. But you know, nobody was goin' to say anything public like. They were nice folks and didn't nobody want to hurt their feelins."

"How old was she when this happened?"

"Oh, I think about 16 or 17. Somewhere about there."

"Well, what ever happened to her?"

"Well, you know none of the local boys would court her, so after she got out of high school, she went to McComb and got a job in a drug store. Met a travelin' man who called on the druggist. Sold drugs for some big company. Wasn't too long before he married her and took her off to live in Memphis. I'd say she done pretty good after all. She musta really been partial to travelin' men."

"Why do you say that?"

"Well, that's where the baby come from."

"Aw, you don't know that. I heard she never told no one who the daddy was."

"She didn't. But I know it was that drummer who came through the summer before, sellin' all sorts of beauty aids."

"I remember him. He had that fancy buggy. Had leather fringe all around. Had a curved dashboard with the design painted on the front with leather paddin' on the top and that fancy black mare pullin' it."

"That's right. All the girls just fell in love with that rig and that drummer would let the girls put on some of his sample cosmetics and then take them out for a ride in that buggy. Sold a lot of stuff that way. Lillie Jean just let him take her for one ride too many."

"How do you know that's what happened if Lillie Jean never told nobody?"

"It came out at the birthin'."

"But you wasn't at the birthin'." And I know old Doc Peters wouldn't talk to nobody about what went on."

"You're right about Doc Peters and you're right that I wasn't there — but Nub Carter was."

"Nub Carter?"

"Yeah. You remember him. Doc Peters would get Nub to drive for him when he had to make night calls. Doc never got enough sleep, so Nub would drive the buggy while Doc slept on the way out and on the way back. And Nub didn't mind talking if you caught him in the right mood."

"And you got the story from Nub Carter."

"That's right. When Lillie Jean's time came late one afternoon, they sent for Doc Peters and Nub drove him out to the Buckner place. She was going strong by the time they got there. Doc got things organized and worked with her for the longest, but the baby just wouldn't come. Lillie Jean wasn't cooperating much and Doc got pretty exasperated with her. Nub said that on the way back into town, Doc was still upset and said that he lost enough sleep because people were always getting sick or hurt through no fault of their own, but he sure hated to lose a night's sleep birthin' a bastard.

"Anyway, Doc had Nub fetching stuff and he was in the bedroom a lot. Lillie Jean was floppin' all about the bed and moanin' and not doin' what Doc was tellin' her to do and Doc finally just got real put out with her. He almost yelled at her, 'Dagnabit, girl! If you'd get yourself in the position you were in when you got this baby, we'd get somethin' done.'

"Nub said Lillie Jean raised her head, looked Doc straight in the eye, and yelled, 'I would, Doc, if I had a leather dashboard to put my feet up on!'"

04
The Aviator Cap

I turned fifty in 1982. For my birthday, my daughter gave me a copy of Eudora Welty's One Time, One Place. The book is a collection of photographs taken by Miss Welty during the early 1930s when she traveled over the state of Mississippi for the WPA. I grew up in Mississippi. Kimberly had recently moved there and begun a new job in Jackson. She was in the process of discovering a Mississippi that she never knew existed.

Miss Welty's photos are mostly of black folk in everyday poses and settings--scenes which I had grown up with, but ones that Kimberly was seeing for the first time. She seemed especially taken with the picture on page twenty-nine of a little Negro boy in an aviator cap. She laughed when I remarked that I had once worn caps just like his. What she didn't, and couldn't, understand was what I really meant when I said that my caps were "just like his."

The little boy is holding a kite, homemade of newspaper. He is wearing a tattered sweater, knickers, and knee socks. The bottom half of the outfit is one that no boy has ever been able to keep together properly for any length of time, and it was obvious that he was having no more success than I had at the same age. One sock is bagging around the ankle, and the elastic on the opposite knicker leg has long since relinquished its grasp on the upper calf and hangs halfway to the ankle like a baggy, cloth stovepipe. But a person who had grown up in that place and time could tell a complete story by seeing only the head encased in the aviator cap.

Aviator caps were popular during the '30s. Practically every boy I knew had one. Aviation itself had caught the popular fancy. Airplanes were not very common in rural Mississippi, and they represented mystery and adventure. When one flew over, everyone would go outside and watch until it disappeared. To a little boy standing there in the Delta mud, that shiny object in the sky represented the ultimate in freedom. When grownups asked, "What do you want to be when you grow up?" I never responded with fireman, policeman, or cowboy. "An airplane pilot" was my standard answer, and with an aviator cap I was one ... at least in my imagination.

Some of the caps were, according to boys who had them, "just like the ones the pilots wear." They were authentic--and expensive. They were made of fleece-lined leather with adjustable straps that buckled under the chin. They came equipped with real leather-framed glass goggles which were held to the cap by an elastic band that passed through a series of loops in the cap's crown. These goggles were normally worn on the forehead and could be dropped in an instant to cover and protect the eyes when the head was thrust from a side window of a moving car or when the wearer was running at breakneck speed across the playground. But most of us had caps like the little Negro boy in the photo. They were either black or brown and were made of some type of imitation leather material on canvas backing. The lining on the other side of the canvas looked and felt like a finish on a cotton flannel shirt. With wear, it rolled up into little balls and rows. The earflaps snapped under the chin. Since I was never too careful with the snapping and unsnapping, one snap usually pulled off, leaving me with dangling flaps which had a bad tendency to curl up, giving the appearance of a fat string hanging beside each cheek.

Whatever process was used to attach the imitation leather to the canvas seldom effected a perfect union. The "leather" usually separated, cracked, and peeled off in odd patterns--a process hastened by cold weather. The goggles were of celluloid, framed by the same material as the cap, and usually came out after a week or two of hard use. They were attached upside-down to the forehead of the cap by three snaps. To position them over the eyes, one had to unsnap them, turn them over, and resnap them. Even the most ill-informed boy knew that any aviator would have been blinded by the rushing wind before this maneuver could have been executed.

At any time the line between rich and poor is a variegated one of many separate yet connected strands. Children see and feel different barriers than do adults. 1 don't remember my parents ever telling me we were poor. They didn't have to. The aviator cap was there for all to see.

But a second-rate aviator cap was better than none at all. And it was always a thrill to get a new cap and have it on when a plane flew over, and to watch the plane through the new, unscratched goggles until it disappeared; and to wonder where it had come from and where it was going, and to wonder what was over that horizon, and to wonder if I would ever get to see either end of the plane's journey.

Some images remain sharp, but, by and large, the memories of those Depression days have been dimmed by the intervening years. Although I never had one then, I've been fortunate to acquire many genuine aviator caps since. They have come in many forms: people, things, events, opportunities, college degrees, accomplishments. Looking at the picture of the little Negro boy and knowing when it was taken, I would judge that we would be about the same age. I can't help but wonder what course his life took and if he ever got an aviator cap in any form.

05
Drummed Out of the Club

Back in the mid-fifties, Morton worked for a large company which had offices in several foreign countries. His job took him to England every month or so and he loved these "business" trips. Through his business connections, Morton became acquainted with several people who ranked fairly high on Britain's social ladder. One of these, Lord Smythe, began to invite him to his gentlemen's club for evenings of dinner and spirited conversations with his circle of friends. Englishmen have long taken special pride in their club associations. Apparently Lord Smythe's London club was one of the more socially prominent ones. It was during these rather frequent visits that Morton struck up a friendship with Lord Bottomley, one of the other club members.

One evening in late winter, Morton was enjoying Lord Smythe's hospitality at his club when he realized that he'd not seen Lord Bottomley. He remarked to his host, "I haven't seen Lord Bottomley this evening. I do hope he's not ill."

A somber look came over Lord Symthe's face as he replied, "No, no, he's not ill. You see, he's no longer with us."

Thinking the worst, Morton asked, "Did he die suddenly? I wish someone had notified me."

"Oh no, nothing like that," responded Lord Smythe as he looked down at the floor, "You see, he was drummed out of the club."

"Drummed out of the club!"

"Yes. It was a terrible situation. The membership voted and Lord Bottomley had to come forward as the drum sounded its ominous cadence. He was stripped of his club tie, scarf, and watch fob and had to walk between a double row of the members out the rear door never to return. Bloody embarrassing, but ol' Bottomley kept a stiff upper lip through it all. I'll have to give him credit for that."

"But why," Morton blurted out, "what could he have done to deserve such treatment?"

As soon as the questions came out, Morton realized their impropriety. This was a private matter. But because of their relationship, Lord Smythe felt obligated to offer some explanation. "Well, you see, Lord Bottomley was having an affair."

"An affair? Was that so bad for this day and time? Haven't you had other members who've had affairs?"

"Well, yes, we have. But you see, old chap, there's just a bit more to it than that. He was having an affair with Lady Ashley, the wife of one of our other club members."

"And for having an affair with another club member's wife, he was drummed out of the club?"

"Well…yes. That and some other things. Lord Bottomley got inebriated at our Christmas party."

"So the drumming out was for having an affair with another club member's wife <u>and</u> getting drunk at the Christmas party?"

"Yes. But there was <u>just</u> a little more to it than that. Not only did Lord Bottomley get inebriated he also went outside and urinated in the snow."

"And that was it? The affair with Lady Ashley, getting drunk, and urinating in the snow?"

"Well, yes. But you see, old chap, there was just a bit more to it that. As he urinated, he wrote his name in the snow."

"Now, am I to understand that Lord Bottomley was drummed out of the club for having an affair with another member's wife, getting drunk at the Christmas party, and writing his name in the snow as he urinated."

"Well, yes. But you see there was something else as well. Lord Bottomley's name was written in Lady Ashley's hand writing."

06
The Sanitary Toilet

Now-a-days it is a joke to refer to a house as having "four rooms and a path." However, it was no joke in the 1930s in Mississippi. Most houses had a "path." This often-traveled thoroughfare usually led out behind the garden or smokehouse around a screen of elderberry bushes to the outdoor toilet. Some of the more cultured referred to it as the "privy" or "outhouse," but my family used the more earthy term "toilet."

It was well that they were generally located away from the main house and hidden from view. In the first place, they were not imposing structures and I've never seen one that would win a prize for architectural design. Upon entering, one would find across the rear an enclosed shelf or bench about two feet off the floor. An oval hole was cut in the top of this, allowing the waste to be deposited on the ground below. Some large families even built "two-holers," but one hole was sufficient for us.

In addition to being not pretty to look at, the toilet also had a terrible smell. It was especially oppressive in hot weather. It was an odor, that once stamped in your olfactory memory, was never forgotten. Late one afternoon fifty years later, I was playing golf and walked up to a green that had just been watered, when that telltale odor flooded my nostrils. Even though we were on a new course in the middle of an upscale residential development, the smell was unmistakable. I remarked that there had to be a toilet close by. My playing partner replied, "No, we use fertilizer on the greens that's made from human waste. It's real good fertilizer, but it smells like this when it's watered." I supposed that some smells were just not meant to die.

Having to walk by a toilet downwind was bad enough; having to be inside one for any length of time was almost unbearable. My grandfather had a book of photographs of World War I which contained several photos of soldiers under gas attack. Those without gas masks were clutching their throats and writhing about on the ground. From my limited experiences, that was the only thing I could imagine being worse than a visit to the toilet on a midsummer afternoon with the temperature hovering at 103 degrees.

One night after supper I heard my parents talking about our getting a "sanitary toilet." This was one of the WPA projects aimed at improving the health of rural residents through improved sanitation. When I asked what a "sanitary toilet" was, Mama replied, "It's one that doesn't stink." Immediately, I knew that was my kind of toilet.

A week or so later a large truck loaded with tools, lumber, and eight or ten men rolled to a stop in our yard. The toilet builders had arrived.

Instead of putting the new toilet somewhere out back and out of view, my father selected a site at the edge of the side yard by the potato patch in full view of anyone passing along the road. After all, a new toilet built by the United States Government was something to be proud of, and worthy to be seen.

The first thing the men did was to dig a pit about six feet square and probably eight feet deep. It's a wonder they kept from covering up my brother Gene and me with the dirt from the pit, since we were so close underfoot watching every detail. I was glad school was out for the summer, so I could observe the whole operation from start to finish.

The pit fascinated me. That was the deepest hole I'd ever seen. I had spent my seven years of life in the Delta of Mississippi where all the land was practically flat. I spent a lot of my time trying to get above it by climbing trees, the ladder to the hayloft in the big barn, and up on numerous outbuildings. The minus elevation of the toilet pit also caught my attention. Little did I realize that it would soon produce a painful experience for me.

After the pit was completed, the workers built a form and poured a concrete slab over it. The slab had a rectangular opening at the rear center. They then proceeded to build the toilet over the slab. The final step was to place the "throne" over the hole in the slab. The "throne" had a hinged cover on top and a vent out the rear of the structure. Screen wire was placed over the vent opening so that no flies could get to the waste, lay eggs, and spread germs. Our "sanitary toilet" was now complete, and an imposing structure it was, made of bright new lumber which contrasted with the deep green of the potato plants.

A few weeks later we experienced a rarity in the Delta summer--a rainy day. Since we could not go outside and play, Gene and I had to find something to do in the house. I got several sheets of paper and began to draw pictures for him. I had completed first grade where we got to draw everyday, so I fancied myself as quite an accomplished artist. My brother was still a year away from starting school and had not been exposed to this advanced instruction. I'd sketch something, and he would try to guess what it was.

Our toilet was still new and much on my mind. I had drawn a front view and a side view of it when I began to think about the pit. Even at that young age, I sometimes tended to see things from a different perspective than other folks. I began to imagine just what one would see if he were down in the pit while the toilet was in use. I proceeded to sketch the scene, being careful to include everything I thought would be observed.

Several times during our drawing session, Gene had taken a picture or two to show to Mama, who was doing housework in another part of the house. So, I didn't think too much about it when he went wandering off with the drawing from the bottom of the pit. I was busily working on another sketch when I heard her voice rise in annoyance and the distinct words, "Where's my switch?" Gene had the ability to get into trouble very quickly, and I just assumed the words were directed at him. It did not register with me that I did not hear any punishment being administered, and so I was still engrossed in my newest drawing when Mama burst into the room waving her peach tree switch around like some demented philharmonic conductor. Before I knew what was happening, she grabbed me up and gave me a severe thrashing while yelling at me about drawing nasty, dirty pictures, and many other words which meant the same thing.

The storm passed as quickly as it had come, leaving me to rub the stinging out of my legs and dry my tears. I wanted to explain that I wasn't trying to be nasty or dirty. I was simply trying to view something that happened every day from a different angle. I didn't see either the act or my perspective of it as things to be ashamed of. But, I knew it would be of no use, so 1 just let bad enough alone.

In looking back on the event, I've often wondered if a budding artist was not sent in a different direction on that summer afternoon. But, more immediately, I received a bigger disappointment--after a couple of months the "sanitary toilet" smelled just as bad as the old one.

07
The Jesus Doctor

In some ways he was just another country doctor. Of course, it was hard to find any other kind in the Mississippi Delta in the 1920s and '30s. With there being hospitals only in the larger towns like Vicksburg and Greenville, the country doctor was always the first, and in most cases the last, medical person anyone would see when illness or injury struck. It would be hard to overrate their importance.

Doc Smith was one of these and, from the many stories I've heard, one of the best. Most of his patients were black farm workers--tenants on the large cotton plantations. Because of his success in treating their many ills, his fame spread by word of mouth throughout this strata of the population. It was among them that he was known as "The Jesus Doctor."

He also enjoyed an excellent reputation in the medical community. When his patients needed an operation, Doc would send them to one of the hospitals in Greenville or Vicksburg. Along with the patient went instructions as to what the surgeon needed to cut on or take out. Early in his practice, the hospitals would run their own tests to confirm Doc Smith's diagnosis. After a time they realized he was never wrong. So they quit wasting time on tests and just followed his instructions. Among these specialists he was said to be the finest diagnostic physician they'd ever known.

Doc Smith was my uncle. He had married Olivia, one of Daddy's sisters. All the kids called him "Uncle Doc," and he was just "Doc" to the grownups. I can't recall ever hearing his first name.

His office was located in Panther Burn. I am told that it got its name from the panthers that lived in the big forests in its early years and from a family named Burn who lived in the area. I'm not sure there were ever any real panthers, but there was probably some type of wildcat around that the early settlers called panthers.

Panther Burn was not a town; it was a plantation village. It was situated on the west side of Highway 61, the old Delta highway, between the highway and the tracks of the Illinois Central Railroad. A wide gravel road bordered by large pecan and oak trees ran from the highway to the tracks. There were two or three houses for plantation supervisors and a large plantation store. Doc's office was situated across from the store near the railroad tracks. It was not his. He had some arrangement with Panther Burn Plantation for its use.

The brown, wood-framed office was not very elaborate. It had two small waiting rooms--one for white, the other for colored--two examining rooms, a small reception area, and a small room filled with medicines. Since there were no drug stores close by, Doc was pharmacist as well as physician. On busy days the large shade trees served as extensions of the waiting rooms.

The majority of Doc's patients came by Greyhound bus or train. Panther Burn was a whistle stop on the railroad and, of course, the bus would stop anyplace along the highway. Patients would generally arrive in the morning, get treated, and catch the bus or train back home in the afternoon or evening. Others might come on foot, by mules, or wagon. It was rare to find a black farm-worker who owned or had access to a car.

Since it was so hard for the blacks to get to him during the week, Doc's office was open all day Saturday and Sunday afternoon. His day off was sometime during the week.

Doc and Olivia lived a couple of miles north of Panther Burn on the east side of Highway 61. They had a nice brick house on five or six acres. They had a large garden, raised chickens, and kept a milk cow as most people did. The house had an indoor bathroom, the first I ever saw.

Olivia was a social climber. Her overriding ambition was to "break into Delta society," and to her, "appearances" were very important. For instance, Doc usually hired someone to milk and tend to the cow. On occasions when the person quit or didn't show up, Olivia had to milk. She would put on a large, floppy hat and baggy work pants and shirt in hopes that anyone seeing her wouldn't recognize her, and then go to the barn before daylight and after dark as added insurance. One morning she did not get an early enough start and one of her friends came by before she finished milking. She hid out in the barn until they left.

Doc was just the opposite. He was just as unpretentious as Olivia was pretentious. His manner was sometimes gruff and abrupt, but he had a soft heart. He liked hunting, fishing, and drinking, and liked being right where he was. He had no desire to "build a big house in town."

"Town" was Hollandale, which was situated about ten miles north on 61. It had two traffic lights and, by the standards of the day, was quite a thriving Delta metropolis. Hollandale was Olivia's residential goal, but Doc resisted for many years.

Olivia attended church in Hollandale where she was a very active member of the Missionary Society. Of course, this was the largest church in town and the one most of the socially prominent families attended. Most of the womenfolk of these families were Missionary Society members as well. Thus, the stage was set for Olivia's Missionary Society garden party. She intended to host an event that Hollandale's social leaders would never forget. She ended up doing just that but not exactly the way she intended.

She recruited Doc and my father to be waiters. They were charged with supervising the food and punch and the several cooks, busboys, and dishwashers Olivia assembled for the event.

The setting was like a picture out of a society magazine; a large, shady side yard surrounded by newly trimmed privet hedges, with perfect weather, white-clothed tables scattered among the trees, and flowers everywhere.

While the women were meeting in the house, Doc, Daddy, and their crew were putting the finishing touches on the food and drink. As they mixed the punch in the large silver punch bowl, Doc would take a sip from time to time. After one of these sips, he remarked, "You know, Luke, this would be pretty good punch if it had about a fifth of bourbon mixed in." As they finished the punch and busied themselves with other preparations, Daddy got to thinking about Doc's comment; and knowing where Doc stashed his liquor, got a bottle of it and managed to get it into the bowl without attracting any attention.

The party itself turned out to be a smashing success. The

food was excellent, the service superb, but the punch seemed to be the crowning achievement. Everyone had to have seconds and thirds and some several cups beyond. They all raved about it and told Olivia it was the best punch they'd ever had. She had not had any herself since she was so busy being hostess, so she had no inkling as to why the punch was so popular.

As the guests were in the process of draining the punch bowl, Doc sidled up to Daddy and whispered, "Didn't I tell you, Luke? That fifth I put in really capped it off." The look on Daddy's face told him the answer to his next question even before he asked it. "Good gosh, Luke, don't tell me you put one in, too?"

Doc knew that two fifths of bourbon had made much too strong a mixture for just about anybody and especially for the ones who didn't drink. But it was too late to do anything about it. He knew they were going to have some drunk women on their hands, and he was right.

Things stayed under control pretty well until the party broke up and the women had to drive home. The first three or four made it down the long driveway and between the gateposts, although one turned left and headed toward Vicksburg and one turned right too quickly and ran off into the bar-ditch beside the highway. A later traveler took down one of the gateposts and a couple of sections of the front fence. Others had a great deal of trouble getting their cars turned about and headed out the drive. They got out into various non-driving areas and several of Olivia's flower beds, shrubs, and small trees became casualties.

Since they had never been drunk before, these women

couldn't understand why their legs, arms, and cars seemed to disobey all rational commands. But it didn't take Olivia long to put together what the cause was. Needless to say, Doc and Daddy were in Olivia's doghouse for a mighty long time.

Doc Smith

In that day and time, all doctors made house calls, and Doc Smith was no exception. In addition to these regular rounds, he was subject to being summoned for emergencies. Since there were no phones in the country, somebody had to come and get him when he was needed to deliver a baby or treat an injury. Doc Smith delivered both my brother and me at home. There was another time when Daddy had to go get him to put me back together. To this day I'm grateful that he was as good a doctor as he was.

We were living on a new-ground farm back in a low part of the Delta toward the river. Because water would cover the land ever so often, our house was built up on pilings about four or five feet off the ground. I was two years old and some months. I don't know just how many. I know that we are not supposed to have memories of things that happen when we're that young, but the incident is still vivid in my mind. I don't remember anything that happened after it but I do remember the fall. I was going up our front steps and something behind me--perhaps a noise, a call, a dog barking--caught my attention. I looked back over my left shoulder but kept on walking up the steps veering to the right as I walked. A step or so from the top I stepped out into space. As I fell, I instinctively threw my right arm out to break my fall. I landed with all my weight on that arm. The elbow splintered, bones came out of the skin and stuck in the soft earth. I remember crying, but I don't remember the pain. Daddy picked me up and sat me up on the porch. Mama came running up and I heard Daddy say, "It's broke. I'll go get Doc." Beyond that, everything about the incident is blank.

Daddy brought Doc back with him and they laid me on the kitchen table. Mama held chloroform to my nose while Daddy assisted Doc. Without the help of x-rays, pins, wires, screws, or all the other things orthopedic surgeons consider indispensable today, Doc Smith took his hands and pushed the broken pieces around until he got them lined up where he thought they should be. He sterilized the gashes where the bones came out, sewed them up, and put on a splint.

When the splint came off, everything seemed to work fine, but my arm was a little crooked. Instead of angling away from my body my forearm angled in. My parents decided to let well enough alone and not attempt any further fixing. Time has proven that decision to be correct. I've thrown just about every kind of ball there is with it and done every kind of lifting and never had a problem, except for having to try to explain to a whole bunch of Army doctors that it really did function. One flatly told me even after I bent it every possible way that any elbow put together that way could not work.

Today, more than sixty years later, when I think about what Doc Smith did that day on that kitchen table, I'm truly amazed. I wonder how many of our modern physicians could duplicate that feat.

Olivia Took Her Place

On those Sunday afternoons when Doc's regular office person was not available, Olivia took her place. She would keep track of the patients and work them in for examinations. If they needed any medicine, Doc would write out what medicine they were to have along with the directions for taking it and give this to Olivia. If the patient or any family member could read, she would type out a label, stick it on the box or bottle, and collect for the medicine and office call. She was performing these duties one Sunday afternoon when the following event occurred.

The train had just stopped, which meant that more patients were arriving. Two or three had come in when a large clamor arose in the colored waiting room. Olivia stepped into the room to be confronted with an unusual sight. A large black woman was leading an entourage of litter bearers who were carrying an even larger black man on a homemade stretcher. With a voice that could be heard in the next county, the woman was shouting, "Let us in, let us in. My man is bad off. We's done brung him a long way to see 'de Jesus Doctor. Oh, please, kin we see 'de Jesus Doctor?"

By this time Doc had come out of one of the examining rooms to see what the commotion was. When the woman saw him, she clasped her hands to her breast and began to wail, "Oh, Doctor, Doctor, please hep my man! We knows dat if anybody kin hep 'im, you kin. Kin you hep 'im, Doctor, kin you hep 'im?"

Doc walked over to the man who had been deposited in the middle of the waiting room floor. He walked around him looking at him from all angles before he said gruffly, "Well, I don't know. He looks to be pretty far gone. But take him in there and put him on the table and I'll see what I can do."

Doc examined him and prescribed some medicine. As he handed the slip to Olivia, he said to the woman, "You give him this medicine, and if he's still alive in two weeks, bring him back." She left clutching the bottle of medicine, leading her small caravan toward the railroad to flag the next train back home.

Olivia was again helping out two weeks later when the man returned. He walked in with his wife who was full of loud praises for "'de Jesus Doctor." When Doc saw them, his greeting was, "Well, I see you didn't die."

"Oh, no sir, no sir," replied his wife. "Jes" look how much better he is. I tol' 'im I knew'd you'd cure 'im if he jes' do what you say. But, Doctor, it ain't been easy. He didn't wanna drink all dat water, but I made 'im. I made 'im drink every drap of it."

The statement about the water puzzled Doc. He picked up the nearly empty bottle of medicine the woman had brought back and read the label. He turned toward Olivia and gave her a look over the top of his glasses that made her blood run cold, for in that instant she realized what she had done.

The directions should have read, "Take two teaspoons three times a day in a glass of water." However, on the day the man was carried in, Doc had seen several women with vaginal infections whose directions for their douche solutions read, "two teaspoons three times a day in a gallon of water." Olivia had mistakenly used those directions and had the unfortunate man drinking a gallon of water at one sitting three times a day.

Doc sat for minute or two and then said to the man, "You're not well yet, but you're going to be. I'm glad to see that you can follow directions and do what I want you to do. I'm going to give you some more medicine, and because you're doing so well, I'm going to cut back on the water."

The man almost fell on his knees in gratitude. "Thank you, Doctor, thank you! I sho 'preciates it. I done had 'bout all the water I wants for a while."

After they left, Olivia said that Doc took her into the medicine room and gave her a chewing out she never forgot. She also admitted that she deserved every word of it. And that was one mistake she never made again.

Coon Hunting With Daddy

Doc Smith liked to fish, but he loved to hunt. He concentrated mostly on deer, quail, and coon. I especially liked it when he went coon hunting with Daddy. He would close his office, make his house calls, and arrive sometime after we had finished supper. He'd go into one of the bedrooms and change into his hunting clothes and bring his "supper" into the kitchen. It was always the same potted meat, vienna sausage, and soda crackers. Mama would give him a big glass of milk to drink, or, if she had churned recently, buttermilk with corn bread. Doc would always share his store-bought supper with my brother and me. We never had things like potted meat or vienna sausage in our pantry, so it was a real treat for us. I often begged Mama to buy some, but she never did, saying it was "just junk made from all the poor and leftover parts of the pig and cow and not fittin' to eat." She was probably right, but her assessment did not reduce my craving for this exotic food.

By the time Doc had finished eating, several more men would have arrived with their coon dogs. Daddy would get Ol' Raymond, our red-bone coon hound, and they would head off to the woods. I never knew when they came back because it would be long after my bedtime, but Daddy would entertain us the next day with stories about the hunt whose dog had run well, how many coons they'd treed, the big ones that outsmarted the dogs, and other related tales.

On one hunt, Doc was unusually fatigued. He'd probably been delivering babies or treating patients for several nights without much rest. After they turned the dogs loose, Doc leaned up against a tree and went sound asleep. The men heard the dogs strike a trail and listened as the coon brought them back in their direction. They got closer and closer and treed the coon about forty yards away. The men went over, shined the coon's eyes, and shot him out of the tree. Then they went back and woke up Doc, who was still leaning against the tree snoring loudly. He was quite embarrassed when he learned that he had slept through the first coon of the evening.

Delta Society

Doc died at a relatively young age. I suppose he was somewhere in his early fifties. Too many long, irregular hours, too many days of non-eating or eating potted meat and crackers, too many 16-hour days combined with nights of hunting or drinking, too much pushing by Olivia to move into town and up in society all took their toll. No one really said what killed him, but I would guess it was his heart combined with any number of other things.

At last, Olivia had her big house in town. Doc had finally given in after the many years of resistance. The house was Olivia's pride and joy. Doc lived less than a year after the move. Perhaps death was a better alternative for him than Delta society.

His body was brought to the new house in a beautiful coffin and placed in the living room. It was there that family and friends would pay their last respects. That's the way it was done in those days. At night the family went to bed, while menfolk, both family members and friends taking turns, sat with the body all night. That's also the way it was done.

On the second morning, Daddy got there fairly early just as Olivia was getting up. He asked her, "Olivia, have you looked out at the back yard?"

She looked rather puzzled as she moved to one of the back windows. "Why no, Luke. What's there to see out there?"

When she pulled the draperies aside, a most unusual picture greeted her. The large back yard was nearly filled with black people-- the farm tenants whom Doc Smith had doctored on for over two decades. They stood in clusters of four or five talking in hushed voices dressed in the clothing of their calling--blue denim overalls, work shirts, blue denim jumper jackets, heavy work shoes or boots. The fine, misty rain ran off the brims of their slouchy felt hats or caps and onto their shoulders, turning the denim a darker shade of blue. Their feet were muddy, and it was obvious that some had walked a long way that morning. They were all in the back yard. In Mississippi in 1940, it would have been improper for a black person to come to the front yard or front door of the white person.

"Now," Daddy said, taking Olivia by the arm, "come look out front." They went to the front bay windows which gave a good view of the street. As far as they could see in both directions, there were other black folk just like the ones in the back yard walking toward the house.

It had not yet dawned on Olivia what was happening. "What do they want, Luke? Why are they coming?"

"Olivia, they've come to say good-bye to Doc."

"But I can't let them come in the house. All that mud would ruin my carpet."

With that, Daddy just about exploded. "What do you mean, you can't let them come in?! I'll go get something to put over the carpet or you can have the carpet cleaned. One thing you're not going to do is deprive them of paying their respects to Doc. You owe them at least that much."

Daddy did cover the carpet with something, and for all that day, Olivia's new house was filled with the people Doc had spent his life helping. They shuffled slowly past the open casket, each one pausing for just a moment. With stooped shoulders, bowed heads, and hats clutched to their chests, they paid their last respects. Some whispered a few words, some moved their lips . . . but no sound came out. Some extended a hand, others just stood silently as tears ran down their weathered cheeks.

The preacher said some nice things about Doc at the funeral. The obituary and article in the newspaper were equally laudatory. His many friends and relatives said some wonderful things as well. But, to this day, I think the greatest tribute paid to Doc Smith was the backyard full of black folk who walked many miles in the mud and rain just to say good-bye to "the Jesus Doctor."

08
A Letter to Kimberly

There is documentary evidence from as far back as the ancient Egyptians and Sumerians of letters written by fathers giving advice and counsel to their children in all manner of life's situations. A few years ago, such an opportunity presented itself to me.

My daughter had recently moved to Jackson, Mississippi, and taken her first professional job as a paralegal in a very old and prestigious law firm. The adjectives "staid" and "conservative" are much too weak to describe it. This firm boasted connections with a U.S. Senator and a former Governor of the State.

Her mother and I were going for our first visit and were scheduled for a tour of the firm and introductions to several of her colleagues. Since this would be our first exposure to them, Kimberly admonished me to be on my best behavior, and to dress properly on my visit to the firm. Wanting to cooperate as much as possible and desiring to help in the furtherance of her budding career, I wrote her the following letter to ease her mind and to reassure her about my appearance.

Dear Kimberly,

I want you to know that I have given some thought to your admonition to "dress properly" when I come to Jackson and meet your associates for the first time. You know that I want to do all that I can to enhance, promote, and further your career. So, in addition to thinking about what course to take, I have been making some preparations. You know how I usually just throw some things together when we make a trip. Well, not this time.

We were out of school last week for spring holidays, and I had time to do some shopping. I decided to do like you women do and get something special for the occasion. After visiting several stores, I happened to drive by Stein Mart. You know, they have a lot of very nice clothes at greatly reduced prices if you have the time to look through a lot of stuff, which I did on that day. I found a nice suit at about one-third of the retail price and bought it. They even had two in my size and I got the conservative one. I asked them to save the remnant when they cut off the pants so that I could send you a piece, but they failed to do so. You know how these big stores are; these salesmen just don't bother to get the word down to the lower echelons where the work is done. Anyway, I'll give you a brief description since I'm so proud of it.

I have never had a suit quite like it before. It's a leisure suit. You know, I thought about buying one when we lived in Knoxville, but never did. It's a polyester double-knit with a 15% cotton blend which gives it a real nice texture. The label says that it is from the "Frederick's of Hollywood Collection." I have not heard of this company, but I feel sure it's a "name" label. You may even see some of their places while you are in California this week. It is dark charcoal in color. I would classify it as a "courtroom attorney, serious case" color. To break the sameness of this dark color, there is just the hint of a light grey plaid in the background. This is so subdued that it is almost sensed rather than seen.

The pants are beltless. They have a wide flap which ends on the left hip when fastened. This gives them a sort of "I don't have to wear a belt" look which really exudes security. The jacket has a belt in the back, which helps to define and accent your figure from the rear. The lapels are saddle-stitched, but they are in good taste. The other one in my size had fancy western stitching around the buttons on the front and sleeves, but I thought that to be just too sporty. The jacket is reversible. The inside is the same color as the muted plaid on the dark side. The plaid on the inside (light side) is charcoal and really stands out. When worn this way, you really have a sporty outfit. Because of this feature, I should be able to get a lot of wear out of this suit. But, don't worry. I only will wear the conservative, dark side out while I'm in Jackson. I'm going to get some new ties to go with it before we come.

I'm sure Sara filled you in on all the news when she wrote this weekend. I just wanted to tell you about my new outfit and how hard I will be trying to make a good impression when we come to Jackson next month.

Love, Dad

The phone rang one evening three or four days after I mailed the letter. After picking it up and saying "Hello," I identified Kimberly's voice saying, "If you do, I'll kill you."

Oh, the pain that can be inflicted by an ungrateful child. I had often heard it said that being a parent is a thankless task and one which is unappreciated by your children. Boy, you can say that again. And since that suit had been altered, I couldn't take it back.

09
" Manday "

Robert taught fifth grade at a small elementary school located in a rural section of the county. Most of his students seldom traveled very far from home. Many had never been to Nashville even though it was only thirty miles away. For that reason he had planned a field trip to that city for them to see the Parthenon, the State Capitol, and several other interesting and educational things.

The trip was scheduled for Friday, so he began to remind them on Monday to bring a dollar to cover the cost of the bus. Most brought their money early in the week. Only a few waited until Friday. Robert was collecting the last few on that morning when Freddie Plunk handed him a note from his mother. It read:

> Dear Teecher
> please let freddie go on the trip. i don't have no doller to send rat now. I will send one on manday.
> cassie plunk

Robert thought she'd just misspelled "Monday," so he put in a dollar for Freddie figuring he would bring it after the weekend.

He suspected that dollars were not easy to come by in the Plunk family. He knew Cassie Plunk was a single mother who did not work. He did not know how she supported herself and her son. Freddie's clothes were always clean and neat even if they were well worn. Robert had met her only a couple of times. He guessed her to be in her mid-twenties and still pretty in a country sort of way. He also guessed Freddie to be the product of a teenage indiscretion.

Anyway, about mid-morning on Monday Robert remembered the dollar. He called Freddie up to his desk. "Freddie, did you remember to bring your dollar today?"

Freddie looked a little puzzled. "No sir."

"Well, I thought the note from your mother said that you'd bring it today."

Freddie still looked puzzled, but then his face brightened, as he understood what the problem was. "Oh, no sir. She didn't say 'Monday.' She said 'manday.' And the man don't come 'til Wednesday."

10
Miss Amy

The land was flat. And to a girl who had lived her whole life in the mountains of north Georgia, almost scary flat like it had somehow gotten out of its assigned place somewhere in Kansas or Nebraska and wandered off, and not being able to find its way home, established itself in the northwestern part of Mississippi. Its flatness was broken only by the trees growing along the creeks and swampy areas which served as the only real dividers between the vast fields of cotton and soybeans. This was "The Delta," and even though I'd seen it before, the first sight of its broad expanse as the road suddenly dropped off the escarpment of the central hills brought the same feeling to the pit of my stomach that it had four years earlier.

Only a month ago I had been a college student, but now I was a graduate and on my way to Greenville and my first "real" job. As I drove westward on a straight road with little traffic, my thoughts wandered to that summer and my first visit to the Delta.

My college roommate was a lifelong resident of this flat country. She insisted that I come and spend a week with her during the summer after our freshman year. This first visit turned into an annual event during our college years. One summer I made a contact which eventually resulted in a job offer and now here I was about to begin a career in business.

But that first visit seemed more special than the rest. I suppose it was because everything and everybody was new and I was doing everything for the first time. We slept late and then spent a goodly portion of each day in or around the pool at the country club. There was a social event of some kind almost every night as Christy's friends seemed to compete for the privilege of having a party with me as the guest of honor. I'd be lying if I said I didn't enjoy all the attention.

But these local parties paled into insignificance when compared to the Delta Ball on Saturday evening forty miles away in Greenville. Young people from all over the Delta--even from as far away as Vicksburg--were there. You see, anybody that is anybody in the Delta knows everybody that's somebody socially speaking, that is.

All the social events had been pleasant, but my mind passed over them quickly, much like a brief ray of sunlight flashing across the landscape during an afternoon thunderstorm. My thoughts came to rest on the visit with Miss Amy. She was dead now. Died during our junior year during mid-term exams. She was a person I knew I'd never forget.

Just to have something to do that summer, Christy was doing volunteer work at her church. One of her assignments was to visit the older members, many of whom were shut-ins. During the week of my stay, she had a mid-afternoon visit scheduled with Miss Amy, and she invited me to go along. I was torn between the visit and the country club pool or really the two boys I'd met who were home from Ole Miss for the summer. Finally, loyalty to Christy won out. However, I almost changed my mind when Christy informed me that we'd have to wear dresses rather than the shorts I'd become so comfortable with. "No one would think of visiting Miss Amy without being dressed properly,"

Christy said with a "proper" almost snob-like tone in her voice.

I pulled a dress out but balked at pantyhose. Christy just shrugged as she pulled hers on and observed, "Maybe Miss Amy won't notice and even if she does, she'll be too much of a lady to point it out." I wondered to myself just what kind of prudish Victorian I was going to see and steeled myself for a long, boring afternoon.

As we drove out to Miss Amy's plantation, Christy filled me in on some of her background. The plantation had been in the family since the early 1800s. Miss Amy was the last of the direct line. She had never married, and had outlived all her brothers and sisters. The best people could figure, she was somewhere in her upper eighties, but no one really knew for sure, and she was not about to tell anyone. And it would be highly improper to ask a lady her age.

Her closest kin were two nephews who ran the 2000-acre spread for her. Upon her death, the place would undoubtedly pass to them. They had built homes close to the large antebellum house in which she still lived.

"Well, here we are," said Christy as she turned the car off the main road onto a graveled lane bounded by two rows of magnolias. Their branches intertwined overhead, which gave one the feeling of driving through a green, leafy tunnel. Only glimpses of the house were visible until we cleared the last pair of magnolias. I let out a gasp as the house, no, the mansion suddenly loomed over us. Scarlett's Tara could not have been more impressive--two tall stories with large columns in front, a red-ribbed metal roof, a shorter wing on one side, a large ell at the rear, surrounded by stately trees that seemed to hold the house prisoner in the embrace of their branches.

As we got out of the car, Christy said, "You'll have to give her your full name. Bev won't do. Miss Amy won't use nicknames or shortened names. Doesn't think that's proper." No one ever called me Beverly Jean except my mother when she was exasperated with me, and I wasn't exactly thrilled by being addressed this way by a total stranger, but I determined to endure everything with as much grace as I could muster.

Before we got across the wide porch, the large screen door was swung open by a tall black man who had obviously been awaiting our arrival.

"Good day, Miss Christine. Y'all come right on in."

"Thank you, Roosevelt. It's nice to see you again."

Roosevelt wore a starched white shirt, black bow tie, dark trousers, and highly polished black shoes. The graying at the temples, the erect posture, and the manner in which he moved conveyed the message that he had been serving in this capacity for many years.

"Y'all come into de parlor while I get Miss Amy. She's spectin' y'all."

He ushered us across the entry hall through a large set of pocket doors into the left front room. After we were seated, he disappeared down the hall toward the rear of the house.

My eyes took a minute or two to adjust from the bright sunlight to the dim interior. No lamps were on. Light was provided by the large windows which were all open, as were the pocket doors between each room. A breeze moved through the house, making it surprisingly cool.

Roosevelt soon returned, escorting Miss Amy. She was a small, slender woman whose step and manner belied her years. Her white hair was done up in a bun at the nape of her neck and her eyes were framed by gold-rimmed spectacles. She wore no makeup on a face that had few wrinkles. She wore a light gray, long-sleeved dress that came down to her ankles. From the way it stood out, I knew she had on more than one petticoat. Old-fashioned lace-up shoes completed the outfit.

"Why, Lillie Christine, how grown-up you're becoming. Thank you so much for coming to spend some time with me." As she spoke, Miss Amy took Christy's extended hand and clasped it into both of hers.

"It's wonderful to see you, Miss Amy," Christy replied. "You're looking great. I do believe you're getting younger."

"Oh, my goodness, girl. You shouldn't flatter a person like that." She dropped her eyes and may have even blushed slightly, but it was evident she enjoyed the compliment.

"Miss Amy, this is Beverly Jean, my roommate from college. She's visiting for a few days."

Miss Amy took my hand just as she had Christy's. Her hands were soft, but the grip was surprisingly strong. She seemed genuinely pleased that we had come to break the tedium of the long summer afternoon.

"Roosevelt, we will take our refreshments in the garden."

Roosevelt bowed slightly and disappeared down the hall.

Miss Amy led us through the house and out a rear door.

A large flower garden took up about half of the large back yard. A brick walkway wound its way through the garden and ended at an elevated gazebo on the opposite side. It was shaded by three large oak trees.

As we were seating ourselves around the gazebo's table, Roosevelt came out through another door carrying a large tray. "I hope you girls like lemonade," said Miss Amy. "I had Essie Mae make some shortbread cookies to go with it." The homemade refreshments were both delicious and plentiful. As we ate, we chatted about a variety of subjects: Where I was from, and what it was like to live in the mountains, what it was like in college these days, how much the crops needed rain, the fire in town last month, the families who had weddings coming up that summer, who had died recently.

Since I had little to contribute to most of the topics, my mind began to wander. When we first sat down, I had noticed the ring. Except for the cameo pin at the collar of her dress, it was the only piece of jewelry Miss Amy wore. It was obviously a diamond, large and square-cut. I could not even begin to estimate its weight, but it had to be several carats. The setting was beautiful and old. There had to be a story behind such a ring. Had it been in the family for generations dutifully being passed down to the oldest daughter? Had it been brought from Europe? Had it been buried under the smokehouse during the Civil War? Had it been used as collateral to save the plantation during hard times?

As she was talking about the new discount store being built on the edge of town, Miss Amy caught me staring at her ring. She stopped talking and seemed to be inviting me to speak. I was so flustered at being caught that I didn't have the presence of mind to consider whether a comment on her ring might be too personal, so I blurted out, "Your ring is beautiful, Miss Amy. Has it been in your family for a long time?"

She did not seem offended by my question but did not answer immediately. Instead, she straightened her fingers, held her hand up at eye level, and turned it so that the ring sent flashes of light out in all directions. You could tell from the faraway focus in her eyes that she was revisiting an event of decades past. The look on her face was one I had seen on the faces of some of my friends who had recently been engaged. I knew what the story of the ring had to be! It was her engagement ring. But the wedding never came about. The young man had died tragically from an accident, or a dreaded disease, or in a war.

Miss Amy's eyes came back to the present and a rather impish look came on her face. Her mouth turned up slightly at the corners in a sly little grin; her eyes sparkled behind the gold rims and I thought I detected a slight wink as she spoke with a candor possessed only by the very young and very old.

"No, dear. You see, one day many years ago, I dropped my drawers at just the right time."

11
Alsey

Alsey was many things, but, first and foremost, he was a teacher of English. He was as comfortable with basic grammar as he was with the Romantic Poets or with modern prose. He loved the beauty and structure of the language as well as the great works written in it. And he had a knack of transmitting this love to youngsters who, at times, did not share his feelings.

Alsey was born and grew up in West Tennessee in the years between the two World Wars. In this era in the South, being educated meant having a broad knowledge of the Liberal Arts. It mattered not whether a person was destined to run the family farm, take over the family business, or enter one of the professions; a foundation in classical studies was considered essential. In this era when relatively few in the South went to college, being "educated" was an important line of demarcation between the social classes.

I first knew Alsey in the later years of his career. His wife was a doctor and the location of her practice determined the location of the family. No matter where her profession took the family, Alsey would secure a teaching position in the local schools and continue his profession. Since his hours were much more regular than hers, he became the cook, the keeper of the house, and the raiser of the children; an arrangement not uncommon today, but one that was unusual forty years ago.

Alsey was a teaching colleague, his wife was our family doctor, and I was privileged to teach their children. In this close association, there were many opportunities to have a lot of discussions with him. I don't think a subject ever came up that he didn't have some degree of familiarity with. During these sessions a great number of stories were swapped. The recounting of a few of these will perhaps illustrate the measure of the man.

Stationed in Germany

Alsey was stationed in Germany right after World War II. He was assigned the task of setting up a school for the children of U. S. soldiers. The war was not long over and just about everything was in short supply. He managed to secure a building which had suffered only minor damage, and an eclectic assortment of furniture which would do for a while until real school desks could be shipped from the States. But textbooks were a different matter. His commanding officer assured him that English texts had been requisitioned and were available at a nearby supply depot.

He got the necessary paperwork together, signed out a three-quarter ton truck with a driver, and headed for the depot. The depot was huge. Our government was in the process of shipping all sorts of material to Germany, and this depot reflected that. It covered several acres. Warehouses held some of the stuff; a lot sat on pallets under tarpaulins; some was just piled out in the open. When Alsey took his forms to the main office, the clerks just laughed at him. They had no English textbooks in their inventory and didn't expect to be getting any. It was apparent that textbooks were well down on their priority list and they did not seem to be disposed to helping Alsey secure any.

Alsey was desperate. He had to have some kind of books. "Don't you have any books?" he asked the supply officer. The officer flipped through several inventory sheets and replied, "Well, we do have a whole room full of Sears and Roebuck catalogs. Why in the world they shipped those things over here, I'll never know." Alsey's face lit up. He asked if he could get some of the catalogs and was told that he could have all he wanted since they were just taking up valuable space. Alsey filled up his truck with them and headed back to his new school.

You see, Alsey had grown up at a time and in a place where many homes had only two books: The Bible (King James version, of course) and the Sears and Roebuck catalog. These two books served not only as a source of moral instruction but also as reading books, dictionaries, and reference books. So, it did not seem so far-fetched to Alsey to use the catalog as an English text. It served him well for a year or so until "real" texts were delivered. You could say that Alsey was a resourceful teacher, a characteristic that did not escape the note of his commanding officer.

Reno, Nevada

During the course of one of our sessions, Reno, Nevada, was mentioned. "Yes, I'm familiar with Reno," Alsey noted, "I spent one summer there a number of years ago."

"What in the world did you do in Reno?" I asked. An impish look came in Alsey's eyes. "I was a gigolo."

I thought my ears were playing tricks on me. "A what!."

"A gigolo."

I had heard correctly, "Aw. Come on. There's got to be a story in that if you can tell it."

"Well, you see it was in the '30s in the middle of the Depression. We had a large farm in West Tennessee and, as you know, cotton farmers in the South were not doing very well. I had gotten in a couple of years of college but it didn't look as if we'd have enough money for me to return. I was determined to finish, but I had to have a summer job where I could save a lot of money. There were no regular jobs to be had close to home, much less summer jobs.

"I was bemoaning this fact in the spring at school when a fellow I barely knew told me about Reno and the amount of money to be made. He said he thought I had the talents they were looking for. With his recommendation and a few letters, I was promised a position for the summer if I could get out there.

"I told my folks that I was going out West to work but I didn't dare tell them what I was going to do. I scraped together what little money I had and got the rest from my father with the promise to pay him back at the end of the summer. I got on a train and headed West. I had to have a job when I got there. There was only enough money for a one-way ticket.

"At that time in most states getting a divorce was difficult. But, Nevada was different. A Nevada resident could get one relatively easily and one only had to reside in the state for six weeks to become a resident. So, Reno became the center of the quick-divorce industry for the whole country. Back then, if you said a woman was going to Reno, it meant divorce. And women were mostly the ones who "went to Reno." And these women mostly had some financial resources. They had to have it if they could afford train fare and a six-week stay at a hotel.

"This was a lucrative business for the hotels and there was considerable competition among them for guests. One hotel room was not much different from another. What attracted women to one hotel or another were the extras, and one very important extra was male companionship or, as I like to say, the quality of that hotel's gigolos. You couldn't expect these women to look at desert sunsets for six weeks. Most wanted to do things and do them with somebody. Consequently, the hotels competed for gigolos about as hard as they did for the women. And here I was, a young college kid from rural Tennessee, pitched into the middle of all this with the stipulation that I do the things I enjoyed doing both day and night and get paid for doing them. If there could be a 'college boy heaven,' this would be it. I took to my work like a duck to water and enjoyed every minute of it at first.

"Indeed, I did have a job. I got a room at the hotel, some meals, laundry service, and small salary. The real money was made in tips. And the better you were at gigoloing, the more calls you got, and the more tips you made.

"Now I hate to brag, but in my younger days, I was skilled at a lot of things. I was a good conversationalist, could play tennis, swim, ride horses, dance, play bridge, only to name a few. Soon, I found myself in great demand because of my versatility. Very early, I observed that most of the women fell into one of two categories, those who enjoyed activities of the day and those who favored the events of the evening. And I was equally adept at both.

"Also, most of my fellow gigolos were only skilled in one area. I quickly saw that I had a significant advantage and I exploited it to the hilt. It was not unusual for me to have an early morning horseback ride with one woman, swim and have lunch by the pool with another, play several sets of tennis with one or two in the afternoon, and have dinner and dancing or dinner and a bridge game into the wee hours of the morning with another.

"This was all fun at first, but I soon discovered that the daytime women liked to do things early and that the nighttime women liked to do things late into the night. I also discovered that a twenty-year-old has some limits and that too much fun for too long begins to be work. But, I was making too much money to slow down. I would go until I couldn't go anymore and then hide out for a couple of days away from my room and phone and sleep and rest up. Then, I'd be back at it again.

"One afternoon late in the summer I was holed up in my room with the phone off the hook trying to get a little sleep. I thought I was dreaming about a loud pounding sound a long way off. It gradually came closer and louder and finally jarred me out of my stupor. Someone was pounding on my door. I staggered over and opened it. There stood my father.

I was too tired to be surprised. He said, 'Son, pack your bag. We're going home.'

"I stuffed my clothes into my suitcase and followed him downstairs. He suggested that I get into the back seat and sleep for a while. Of course, it was as hot as blue blazes, but I slept all the way to Arkansas. That's a long way on two-lane roads. Just look at the map.

"My father never did say how he found me, but I found out later that a woman from our town had been to Reno that summer for a divorce. I never saw her, but she must have seen me and then told someone when she got back. I guess the word eventually got to my father, who headed west to redeem his prodigal.

"My parents never said much about that summer. But I knew not to try it again. Anyway, all that riding, tennis, dancing, and bridge paid for my next year of college. Looking back, it wasn't a bad trade-off."

Teacher Workshops

"I used to do a lot of workshops. I enjoyed doing them and, at one time, I was in demand. Not as much as I was in Reno as a gigolo, but not bad for an older fellow.

"A school system would have a day of in-service education for their teachers and invite 'experts' from other places to come and lead sessions in their particular fields. I worked up several presentations on various aspects of teaching English and began to get calls from systems around the mid-state to be a presenter. The usual format was three sessions before lunch with visiting presenters and the afternoon with local work. Usually, I was asked to do one or two sessions which gave me some opportunities to sit in on other presentations.

"On one occasion I was invited to participate in a workshop in another county. I was only doing one session which was scheduled first. I intended to do my presentation, attend two others, have lunch, and drive home.

"Everything went very well at the beginning. I thought that I did a pretty good job with my presentation, but I did not realize just how good I was. As the session ended, the teacher who was responsible for the English sessions rushed up to me just gushing about my presentation, how wonderful it was, one of the best she'd ever heard, etcetera, etcetera. She insisted that I stay and present it again at the next session so that more people would have the opportunity to benefit from it.

"Of course, I was flattered and figured that I had been underrating myself. I agreed to do the second session.

"As I closed out my second presentation, she came rushing up again. The first round of compliments could not hold a candle to this second set. It was the best she'd ever heard, a seamless tapestry of wisdom and intellect, etcetera, etcetera. And I just had to do it again. She would not accept no for an answer.

"My chest swelled out (along with my head) and I felt a distinct calling to stay and share my expertise with those who were obviously less fortunate. How could an education missionary do less?

"After my third presentation, she praised it as she had the others and thanked me profusely. I left so swelled up with pride that I did well to fit through the front door of the school.

"I went down to the town square to have lunch. The cafe was the type that can still be found in the center of most towns in Middle Tennessee. It was old with those large, high-backed booths along one wall. I chose a booth and was looking over the menu when three or four women came in and took the booth in front of mine. From their conversation I gathered that they were local teachers who had been to the workshop that morning. This exchange came soon after they sat down:

'Well, how did your morning go?' 'Terrible!' (I recognized the voice of the English coordinator who had been praising me all morning.) 'Really? What was so bad about it?' 'Only one of my presenters showed up. If it hadn't been for that little fat man from Shelbyville, I wouldn't have had any program.'

"Talk about getting a deflation. I went from ten feet tall to about a foot or less. I felt like I should ask for a child's booster seat so I could reach the table to eat. You know it says in the Scriptures that we are not to think of ourselves more highly than we ought to think. I'm telling you, I learned that lesson that day."

* * *

During his long career, Alsey taught in several schools. One of his stints was teaching fifth grade in a rural school in the bootheel of Missouri. It was during this time that the "new" idea in education was to take a single topic and develop it into a unit in which all the subject areas were taught. Alsey did not much care for this concept and was not bashful about letting his feelings be known. But, this "new" concept was being pushed by the central office, and Alsey's voice was but a small one crying out from the wilderness. In order to get the implementation underway, it was decreed that each teacher would develop one unit that first year.

At one big in-service meeting on this "new" concept, a number of teachers were stating the units they intended to develop. When Alsey's turn came, he said with a mixture of flippancy and sarcasm, "My class will make homemade ice cream." His pronouncement received mixed reviews, with disbelief and ridicule being the more prevalent. The administrator from the central office said it couldn't be done, and most of his colleagues laughed at such a silly idea. This made Alsey even more determined to carry out his plan.

He worked hard and long researching his topic and producing a good teaching unit. In social studies, the class studied the history of ice cream, its geographical spread through the world, and which social classes had access to it and why they did. In math, they worked on the measurement of the ingredients. For science, the class learned about freezing points, how the salt lowered the freezing temperature of the ice, how the gears worked in a hand-cranked freezer, and why the canister of a freezer should only be filled to a certain point before freezing. In language arts, they learned new vocabulary words and how to spell them, as well as writing stories about ice cream.

All of this was looked at very closely by the central office and they seemed pleased with Alsey's unit. But, as Alsey said, "The day came when we had to make the ice cream." And he was right to be fearful of the act itself.

Alsey could be creative and thorough with the "book" parts of the unit, but he had a pretty good idea of what would happen when he mixed several hand-cranked freezers, milk and other ingredients, salt, and ice with about thirty excitable fifth graders. And his worst fears were realized.

To compound things, almost the whole central office staff came to visit his class to witness the grand culmination of the ice cream unit. In the process, the children got milk, sugar, salt, ice, etc., on or in just about everything in the classroom. Alsey said that he thinks some ingredients actually got on the ceiling and dripped on those below.

After what seemed like an eternity, the ice cream was made and the time came to eat it. As this phase was beginning, one little girl got too eager and ate too much too fast. She jumped to her feet, pressed one palm to her forehead, and exclaimed in a loud voice, "Oh, I's got a misery in de haid!" At that Alsey stood, asked for the class' attention, and responded. "Boys and girls, this is our health lesson with this unit. If you eat homemade ice cream too fast, it will give you a misery in your head." The central office folks loved it.

Although Alsey received high marks for his unit and for his creativity, he was careful not to make that kind of mistake again. He spent the rest of the year getting his room and its furnishings cleaned up from the ice cream unit.

The last time I saw Alsey he was struggling to recover from a serious stroke and he would not live much longer. The stroke had taken his mobility but, worse than that, it had robbed him of real speech. Gone was that wonderful flow of words and stories in that accent of a true southern gentleman. Halting and uneven phrases were the best he could do. But his eyes were alert and seemed to be trying to say, apologetically, that the real Alsey was still there. He had just been locked away inside.

Yes, Alsey was a teacher. But he also had a reach and touch beyond a classroom's confining boundaries. This part of the world is better because he passed through it. Could a better thing be said of anyone?

12
Christmas Stories

The Christmas Orange

It was the Sunday just before Christmas Day and my Sunday School lesson dealt with gifts and gift giving--an appropriate as well as a timely focus. As an introductory exercise, I had asked each member to think of a Christmas when they were children and when they had received a very special gift. Next, I asked each of the men to share with the class things they remembered about this gift. What it was, why it was so memorable, and so on.

The things that were shared were good but fairly predictable: the first bicycle, tricycle, football uniform, fishing rod, rifle, and so on, down the line. But, then it became Bryan's turn. When he stated that the most memorable gift of his early years was an orange, he got everyone's attention.

I had known Bryan for several years and knew that he had grown up on a small farm in East Tennessee. We were about the same age, which would have placed his childhood in the Depression years of the 1930s. The dire economic straits of this section of the state were common knowledge, but I had no clue as to his family's standing on the economic ladder. He was certainly educated with a doctorate in agriculture from the University of Tennessee. In fact, he was employed by the University and worked with their statewide agricultural program. So, I was as taken aback as the rest when the statement about the orange came out.

"An orangel" repeated one of the members, his voice rising at the end in an incredulous question mark.

"Yes, an orange," replied Bryan. "Let me tell you why.

"Some of you know that I grew up in East Tennessee no, make that rural East Tennessee. The road in front of our house was dirt. We were about a mile off the main road, which was made of rock. We lived on a small farm. My dad was a good farmer and he farmed hard, but there wasn't much bottom land and you can't get much to grow on those rocky hillsides. It was bad enough in normal times but in the Depression it was much worse. We weren't just poor; we were pore. Fortunately, Dad raised enough to feed us so that we didn't go hungry, but we never had much money.

"Well, one year as Christmas approached, Mama sat us kids down (I was about 6 or 7) and told us that there would be no Christmas presents that year. She said that there was just no money. Of course, we were all disappointed, but we understood as well as kids of that age could. Even when there were gifts, we usually got only one each and it was always an item of clothing. I think the year before I got a flannel shirt.

"As the Day drew near, I tried not to think about it. I didn't blame my parents. I knew they were doing the best they could, but that knowledge couldn't keep a hollow feeling from swelling up in my chest every now and then.

"On Christmas Eve, my dad walked down to the little country store on the main road to get some meal and flour and other staples. The owner let most of the people in the community have things on credit. He went by himself. He said it was too cold for us to walk that far.

"I really didn't want to get up the next morning. There would be no gift to open and that feeling was in my chest and I couldn't make it go away. But, when Mama called us to breakfast, we didn't have the choice of staying in bed. I got up slowly and reluctantly pulled on my overalls and headed for the warmth of the kitchen.

"As I entered, I bumped into one of my older brothers who was standing just inside the door. I wondered why he hadn't gone to his place at the table. Before I could figure this out, the other kids came pushing in. It took a few seconds for us to get ourselves sorted out and to see just what had stopped my brother in his tracks. My dad was seated at his place, Mama was taking a large pan of biscuits out of the old wood stove, and there at each place at the table was an orange. They were shiny and seemed to glow as they reflected the light from the coal oil lamp in the center of the table. We did get a gift for Christmas after all!

"We rushed to the table as one and snatched up our treasures. We rubbed them, smelled them, and compared sizes and shapes with each other. This initial excitement lasted for several minutes before we could even discuss when would be the best time to eat them. It was finally decided that there would not be a better time than right then. As we peeled them, the whole kitchen was filled with the wonderful aroma. Even today, I cannot smell a fresh orange without remembering that Christmas morning.

"On his trip to the store on Christmas Eve, along with the flour and other stuff, my father had bought six oranges one for each member of the family. Years later after I was grown, he told me, 'I was determined that my family have something for Christmas.' All six probably did not cost more than twenty-five cents, just a few pennies. But every penny is precious when you don't have any.

"That spring my father got a job doing road work for the county, with a regular pay check. That meant that we would get real gifts for Christmas from then on. But, because the oranges had meant so much to us, we started off the day with them the next Christmas. It became a family tradition, one that I've continued in my present family. Before we look at any other gifts on Christmas morning, we all gather around the kitchen table and eat our oranges. It helps to bring Christmas into better focus and helps us all think about the small things that help so much to make Christmas a reality."

Sleigh Tracks

One of the fond memories I have of my father centers around an incident that happened one Christmas before I was born. My cousin, Donald, who was involved in the story, related it to me after my father's death. It occurred in the late 1920s when Donald was about eight years old.

It seems that Donald had decided that there was no Santa Claus and had proceeded to let everyone know how knowledgeable he had become about the source of Christmas toys and candy. The adults pointed out to him just how wrong he was, but he would not be dissuaded.

As darkness fell on Christmas Eve, it was cold and snow began to fall. By bedtime it was apparent that there would be a good layer on the ground on Christmas morning. A snowfall in December was a rare occasion in Mississippi, and this one came at a fortunate time.

My father was one of the adults who had been trying to show Donald the error of his thinking about Santa Claus. Dad was known for his practical jokes and the tricks he often played on people. The timing of the snow and Donald's disbelief undoubtedly set his mind to working.

As the children were being readied for bed, my father said to Donald, "I know you say that you don't believe, but Santa Claus is coming tonight. You've seen the gifts he's left for you every year and in the morning you'll get to see his tracks in the snow. Most people say that Santa lands on the roof in his sleigh, but your roof is too steep. He will land out in the side yard where it's flat and where there's plenty of room. In the morning when you see the tracks of his sleigh and reindeer, you'll know that Santa is real."

Donald went to bed with a know-it-all smirk on his face, but there may have been just a little doubt in his mind.

After going through his presents the next morning and finding some from Santa Claus, Donald went out on the side porch to check out the truth of my father's bedtime words. Sure enough, there they were--sleigh and reindeer tracks. They were out in the middle of that big yard with an expanse of unbroken snow on all sides. He could see where the sleigh had landed and taken off again. It had to have come from the sky. The unspoiled snow everywhere else testified to that fact. There really was a Santa Claus.

For at least three more years, Donald was a true believer. After all, he had seen evidence that few others had.

When Donald got older, he figured out that my father had to have been responsible for the sleigh tracks. However, Dad never admitted it to him. In fact, so far as I know, my father took this secret to his grave. He never admitted it to anyone, or told anyone how he pulled it off. But, on that snowy Christmas he did make a real believer out of one eight-year-old boy.

Caroling

There are some things a person just misses out on when they grow up in the country. Caroling is one of them. In the first place, there was so much distance between houses that the singers would have had to form a caravan to get around. In the second place, the area was so thinly populated that if a group had gotten together to carol, there would have been no one at home to sing to. Oh, we had all seen pictures, read stories, and heard about it on the radio. Many of us just never had a first-person experience with it.

But all that changed after I got married and came to reside in a small town in Middle Tennessee. The town was small enough for a group of carolers to cover the whole town on foot. And there were plenty of people to sing to. A large segment of the population was made up of elderly couples and widows who were almost always at home after dark. One Christmas, a group of adults from our church decided to get together and go caroling to them. I was looking forward with great anticipation to my first caroling experience. And quite an experience it turned out to be.

Well, as fate would have it, the weather turned cold--real cold . And it was getting colder by the day, but we were not to be deterred. On the appointed day, we set off at dark bundled up from head to toe. The temperature was about 20 degrees and falling.

We didn't have songbooks or song sheets. Back in this time, practically everyone knew at least the first verse of just about every Christmas carol. We would walk up to the front porch, someone in the group would call out the title of a carol, and we'd sing a verse or two. Then someone else would call out another, and the process would be repeated. Usually, the residents would come out on the porch, and after we had sung four or five selections, someone would ask them if they had a favorite they'd like to hear. If so, we would sing it and then visit with them a few minutes, wish them a Merry Christmas, and be off to the next house.

By the time we had been to four or five houses, we could see a pattern developing. When asked if they'd like to request a favorite carol, they would usually say, "Oh, no, just sing anything." Now, one lady in the group really loved "Silent Night." So when there was no specific request, Catheran would ask quickly, before anyone else could say anything, "Would you like to hear 'Silent Night?'" Of course, they would reply with something like, "Oh, yes, that would be nice." Whereupon Catheran would announce to the group, "All right, they want to hear 'Silent Night.' Let's sing it for them."

After this happened several times, it began to strike most of us, especially the men, as rather humorous. As the pattern continued to be repeated at every house, a few snickers could be heard when the "request" for "Silent Night" was made.

When we got to the home of the Tuckers, we went around to the back because everyone knew that they lived mostly in the long ell that ran off the front rooms. The ground dropped off toward the back of the lot, making the ell stand fairly high off the ground. In fact, the porch back there was elevated about five feet. The house was an old one with long windows that came all the way to the floor.

We clustered ourselves in front of the steps and began to

sing. I was on the left edge of the group directly in front of the only lighted window. The window shade did not come all the way down, affording me a good view of the Tuckers' bedroom. Mr. Tucker was in bed but not asleep. Mrs. Tucker was sitting in a rocking chair in front of the gas heater doing some needlework. We had just about finished our first carol before it dawned on them that there were carolers at their back door. Mrs. Tucker got up and headed for the door. Mr. Tucker threw back the covers, sat up, and swung his feet to the floor. He had on a one-piece suit of long underwear. As he put his feet into his slippers, he got his hat from the bedside table and put it on. He pulled his pants off the back of a nearby chair and got into them before standing up and pulling his suspenders up over each shoulder. By the time we finished our second carol, Mrs. Tucker had come out on the porch. She was not aware that her husband was getting ready to put in an appearance.

After everybody greeted everybody, someone asked about Mr. Tucker. "Oh, he's already gone to bed," Mrs. Tucker responded. At just that moment, Mr. Tucker appeared at the door behind her. He had not donned a shirt. The top portion of the suit of underwear served in that capacity. And his misshapen felt hat sat on his head at a jaunty angle. Catheran, who in addition to loving "Silent Night," also was noted for saying just about whatever came to mind, blurted out in a voice loud enough to be heard in the next town, "My goodness, does he sleep in his hat?" We all got a good laugh out of it and the Tuckers didn't seem to be offended. We sang three or four more carols, ending with the always "requested" "Silent Night."

We stopped at several more houses without incident. Of

course, "Silent Night" was the concluding piece at all of them. It was like we were following a Sunday morning order-of-service, and it was getting funnier with each repetition.

By this time we were really feeling the effects of the cold. My feet no longer had any feeling in them, and I'm sure a majority of the others were equally uncomfortable. Most were ready to head for the warmth of the church and some hot chocolate. But we pushed on doggedly to the Stephens' home at the end of the street. We found it hard to get close to the front porch of this house. There were large shrubs all along the front. A brick walk led up to the front steps, but it was narrow with about six or seven foot-tall boxwoods on both sides. We formed up along the walk for our concert with the women in the front and the men in the rear. Mr. and Mrs. Stephens came out on our second carol. Mr. Stephens reached up and pulled the string to the porch light which was a bare bulb on a drop cord. The bulb must have been 200 watts. Its blinding rays cut through the cold darkness like London searchlights during World War II. After a couple more carols, one of the women asked if they wanted to request a favorite carol. Back came the standard reply, "Oh, we like them all. Just sing anything." Before Catheran could speak, our young minister who was back amongst the men raised his hand and asked in a plaintive, almost servile voice, "Ma'am, would 'Silent Night' be all right?" Well, that was like the small stone that triggers an avalanche. All the men became convulsed with laughter. Of course, the Stephens agreed with the selection, and the women began to sing "Silent Night."

I was laughing as hard as the rest and made the mistake

of moving to the edge of the sidewalk which was not flush with the ground, but raised about two inches. My frozen feet weren't functioning too well anyway, and when I stepped on the edge of the brick, my ankle rolled, throwing me into the boxwoods. My hands were deep in my coat pockets and could not be extracted with any speed, so I had no way to break my fall. I went in head-first like a large harpoon. The branches then imprisoned my arms, making it impossible for me to get my hands out. So, there I was, upside down in a big bush and unable to extricate myself. The men thought this was even funnier, and it caused a significant increase in the volume of the sounds coming from the male members.

I had ceased to see the humor in the situation, but later when one of my fellow carolers described the scene to me, it was not hard to fathom. The women were trying to stand straight with some decorum as they sang a rather ragged version of "Silent Night"; the men were falling all over each other with their laughter practically drowning out the singing; and one bush in the back was waving around like it was being attacked by a Florida hurricane. The Stephens were craning their necks around and shading their eyes from the bright light as they attempted to see and to figure out exactly what was happening on their front walk.

A couple of the men finally laughed themselves out enough to find the strength to drag me out of my leafy prison and set me upright. I was wearing so many clothes that nothing was injured except my dignity. By mutual consent we made the Stephens' place our last stop.

I still enjoy hearing the carols of Christmas and I think "Silent Night" is a beautiful song. I cannot hear it without remembering that cold night in front of the Stephens.

The Yellow Umbrella

I really don't want to go, was the thought that kept running through my head. This was the first year I'd felt that way. I suppose the cold rain had something to do with my reluctance. It wasn't raining hard. Just a steady drizzle. Just hard enough to make everything messy and driving difficult. And even though the actual temperature was only in the 40s, the cold seemed to penetrate to the bone. *Typical Middle Tennessee Christmas weather,* I thought. *I really don't want to go.* But I continued driving.

It was only late afternoon, but the low rain clouds and the time of year made it as dark as midnight. Four days before Christmas and I still had some last-minute things to get done. *Why did I volunteer for this anyway? I'd volunteered the last three years and some had yet to volunteer. Why couldn't this be one of them driving through the rain and heavy traffic? I really don't want to go.*

I thought about my husband who was just coming in from work as I was leaving. He would now be eating his dinner I'd left on the stove and would probably spend the rest of the evening sitting in front of the fireplace with a good book. That was much more inviting than what I'd be doing.

The Christmas lights reflected off the wet cars and wet streets. I suppose it was pretty, but I was not much in the spirit to see the beauty. I still had some Christmas preparations to make. *Why couldn't I be doing them rather than giving a whole evening for something else? Why couldn't I be at home with my husband in our cozy den? Why did I volunteer? If I had known what this night would be like back the first of*

November, I'd never have put my name on that list.

No, I didn't have any of the so-called "Christmas spirit." I resented what I was doing and was doing it only out of a sense of duty or guilt, or maybe some other emotional feeling I couldn't define. I'd thought about turning around two or three times but hadn't seen a good place when the thoughts struck me. Anyway, it was too late to go back now; my destination was only a half-block away. I turned in and parked. Not many cars tonight. It was still raining.

A large, hand-lettered sign was taped to the inside of the front window. Each letter was drawn on a separate piece of poster board. It said simply, "THE MANGER."

Until a few weeks ago, the building had been an empty store. The owner had donated it for our use. It was stocked with a wide assortment of items contributed both by local businesses and by individuals. It was a place for the needy to come and "shop" for Christmas. But it wasn't for just anyone who wanted to come by. Families had to be screened by local agencies before being issued a letter of authorization.

The Manger was staffed by volunteers from local churches and civic clubs. This was one of the community projects in which my Sunday School class participated. We'd been doing this for several years and each member was encouraged to volunteer for at least one night. Some couldn't, but most did. Margie, our class president, was one of the Manger's organizers and was on hand several nights. She'd probably be here tonight. I got out of the car, put my umbrella up against the drizzle, and went inside.

As I was in one of the back rooms putting away my coat

and umbrella, Margie came in. "Well, good evening, Susan," she said cheerfully, "I'm really glad you could make it. Some couldn't, so we're a little short on help. But it looks like the rain is going to keep our crowd down, so we'll probably be ok."

How could anyone be so bubbly on a night like this? "Well, I'm here," I replied. The gloom and self-pity must have been evident in my voice, because Margie came over and put one arm across my shoulders. "Come on, old girl, this is going to be a great night. Just you wait and see," she said with a tone of encouragement in her voice. I was not convinced and just grunted as she left the room.

As I made my way to the front door to await my first shopper of the evening, I passed the jewelry counter. I hoped that I wouldn't get a shopper who spent most of the time selecting gaudy jewelry rather than looking for the practical items I knew they must need. The store really is a good deal for these folk. Large gifts are a dollar; small gifts are fifty cents. The theory is that there is dignity attached to their actually buying something for someone, even if it is at a greatly reduced price. Everything else (clothes, books, household items, etc.) is free.

It takes a number of volunteers to run the store, mainly because each shopper is escorted and assisted by a volunteer from entry through check-out. If more shoppers came than Margie anticipated, it would probably be a frantic evening.

There was only one volunteer ahead of me at the front door a man whom I didn't know. Just as I walked up, an elderly couple came in and showed him their letter. He took it, got a shopping cart and left, headed for the household goods. The next one would be mine. I wondered what I'd get.

I saw the girl before she got inside. With no raincoat or umbrella, she reminded me of a lost puppy looking for shelter from the rain. She stopped just inside the door and shook the excess water off her clothes and hair. She was clean and neatly dressed, obviously doing the best she could with the clothes she had. I was taken aback by her obvious youth. She couldn't be more than 18 or 19, about the same age as my daughter who was away in her first year of college.

As she fished her letter out of her purse, she realized I was standing there watching her. She looked up and her eyes sparkled as her face broke into a broad smile. "Hi. I'm Angie. Are you going to help me?" she asked holding out the letter.

"It sure looks that way," I replied rather listlessly. I took the letter, glanced at it, and moved toward the row of shopping carts. "Where do you want to start?" She didn't seem to be put off by my obvious lack of enthusiasm and brusque manner.

"Let's do clothes first. I've got my list all made out for everybody." Angie took a piece of paper out of her purse and unfolded it. The deep creases and smudges told me that it had been folded and unfolded many times. "I've been working on it ever since we got approved, so I could make sure I got everyone something nice." She was still smiling, and the anticipation in her voice was almost that of a child who was close to being turned loose in an ice cream parlor with no restrictions on how much she could eat. I was struck by the incongruity of the situation. Water still dripped from the ends of her blond hair. Her feet had to be wet in those worn tennis shoes. She had to be chilled to the bone in the damp clothing. And yet, there was that bright smile and the lilt in her voice. I wondered to myself if she were just putting on a good front for my benefit.

As I got a shopping cart and headed for the clothing section, Angie began to talk. "I hope I'm not too late to get the things I want. I've been trying for over a week to get a night off. I work the early night shift at the Big-Sak store over on Westgate. My boss said he'd put me on daytime, but there's nobody to look after my kids until my husband gets home."

Kid, I thought to myself. *Why this little girl is hardly more than a kid herself*.

We arrived at the clothing section. Angie unfolded her list. "My husband's right at the top," she said. I couldn't help but notice the loving tone in her voice. "He works outside most of the time and really needs something warm. Oh, this will be just the thing," she said as she found a lined, denim work jacket in his size. She continued to make similar comments as she picked out a pair of steel-toed work boots, a shirt, and two pairs of pants. She went through the tables and racks of clothing with an efficiency and skill that belied her age.

After carefully stacking her selections in the rear of the cart, she again consulted her list. "Bobby's next. He's my older brother. He's 19, the same age as my husband. He's not working too regular now. He really likes this cowboy stuff," she said as she went through a rack of western boots and found his size.

"Katie needs a real heavy sweater. She's my little sister. She's 16 and in the tenth grade over at Southside. You know, Katie's kinda funny in the head about some things. Won't wear a coat in the winter. Just sweatshirts and sweaters."

By the time the monologue on Katie was finished, Angle had found what she was looking for and had placed it in the cart.

"My kids are pretty well off with clothes right now. James Jr. is three and Alice is almost two. But they really need some caps and gloves to wear when they play outside." These were found and added to the growing pile.

"Daddy really doesn't need any clothes," Angle said almost to herself as she surveyed the racks and tables. "Doesn't go out of the house too much anymore. The doctors say he's got some sort of mental problem, but they don't say just what. Whatever it is has gotten worse since Mama died a coupla years ago. Mostly just sits and stares. Don't bother nobody. Just sits.

"But," Angle said, her voice rising a little, "he does like to fish. The water seems to soothe his mind. Do you think there might be a fishing rod I could get for him?"

"Let's go over to the sporting stuff and see," I replied. That my voice now had some enthusiasm in it surprised me. For some reason I was beginning to feel better. And I really wanted to find a fishing rod for her dad, but there was not one in the whole section. I even looked under all the tables and behind the cabinets, but there was no rod of any kind to be had. I was disappointed and it must have showed. "Oh, that's all right," said Angle cheerfully, "I'm sure I'll be able to find something else he'll like."

"What's next?" I asked.

"Books and puzzles for James and Alice."

Angie continued to talk as I guided our cart toward the book tables. "I try to read to them everyday, but they get tired of the same stories over and over. I'm told that reading to them will make them learn better. Do you think that's true?" She hardly paused long enough for me to nod my assent. "It's hard some days to find reading time, but I don't miss many. I want them to learn more than I did in school. I didn't finish. I want them to finish."

Angie stopped abruptly as we were passing a large stack of knitted afghans which had been donated by one of the local industries. They were all new and fresh looking in their clear plastic wrappers. "Aren't these nice? They'd be just the thing for us to wrap up in this winter when we're watching TV. You know, it's not real warm in our house when the wind blows. Could I have more than one?" There was a pleading note in her voice.

"I don't see why not. How many would you like?"

"Could I have as many as ... four?"

"Of course you may. That's what they're here for." She selected four in different patterns, and I helped her stack them on the bottom rack of the cart.

Before we could continue our journey, Angie spotted a new dish drain on a nearby table. "Oh," she exclaimed excitedly, "this would be just right for Daddy. He washes all the dishes every meal. He really likes to do it. I think it's the water thing. He seems contented when he's got water on his hands. His old one will hardly hold the dishes anymore." I found a place for the drain on top of the afghans.

Angie was even more excited at the large number of children's books. I helped her pick out about a dozen or so, making sure that she got a variety of stories. And she wanted puzzles with big pieces so the kids could work them. A diligent search through the puzzle boxes turned up three that filled the bill. "And I need a dictionary," Angie said. "I have to look up a lot of words and I want to teach my kids about using one." I had to turn over a lot of books before I located one.

"What about some toys?" I asked. "You know it really wouldn't be Christmas for your children unless they got some toys."

"I know. And I want them to have some . . . but not too many. And I don't want any guns or war toys or any with small pieces they can swallow."

"You know, Angie, you're really a good mother."

Her eyes seemed to light up even more. "Really? No one has ever said that to me before."

"I can't understand why not, because you are."

In the toy department we searched through almost the whole selection to find just the right ones to meet Angie's expectations. During this process a feeling began to well up in me that I had not felt for a long time. It was the same feeling I'd had many years ago as I'd picked out toys and things for my children. It's funny how you don't forget those things.

The last thing Angie did was to make some very careful

selections in the "pay-for" gift department.

The cart was now piled high as we headed for the check-out lane. I was pleased to note that she had not given the jewelry counter even one look. Her gift total came to nine dollars. She handed the cashier a ten dollar bill. As the cashier started to hand her the dollar change, Angie put up her hands in protest and took a step back. "Oh no, I don't want any change. You all just keep the dollar and use it for those who can't afford to pay."

I turned my head quickly so that Angie couldn't see the tears welling up in my eyes. Her last statement had touched a nerve somewhere down deep--a nerve I didn't know I had. She didn't seem to notice.

As I pushed the cart to the door, I noted that the heavy drizzle had not slackened any. "You really need something over your head," I said.

"Oh, I'll be all right."

"No," I protested, "you've got to have something. You stay right here and let me go over to the umbrella rack and get you something to keep that rain off."

I hurried over to the rack only to find the pickings extremely slim. There was only one umbrella left a bright yellow lady's model which had seen better days. The fabric had come loose from the end of one of the ribs and two of the ribs on the opposite side were bent downward at odd angles. But, since it was the only one, I took it back with me along with apologies for its condition.

"Aw, this'll do just fine. I'm not big enough to need very much." Angie opened the odd-shaped thing and bounced it up and down like some little girl with a summer parasol. "Thank you so much for helping me. We're going to have a great Christmas this year!" she exclaimed as she looked at the piled-up shopping cart. "I hope you have a good one too." As our eyes met, I sensed a depth of understanding I'd not seen before.

"I think...no, I know I will now," I replied. "Merry Christmas, Angie."

I held the door open for her and she pushed her cart out into the rain. She was still smiling that bright smile as she guided the cart with one hand, while bobbing the umbrella up and down in the other.

I stepped back inside the door and stood watching as the yellow umbrella marked her progress down toward the few remaining cars. The tears were flowing faster now and burned my cheeks. I wiped at them half-heartedly.

"What do you see out there, Susan?" Margie's voice startled me.

"I'm just watching Angie leave," I replied as I turned toward her. But Margie didn't look at me. Her eyes were on the parking lot. She craned her neck for additional height and moved her head from side to side to get a better view. Her brow furrowed with concern. "There's no one out there," she said.

I snapped my head back around. Margie was right. The yellow umbrella was gone, along with Angie and the shopping cart. The only movement was the cars passing along the main street. My head had only been turned for four or five seconds. I didn't see how it was possible for her to have gotten into a car that quickly.

"Did you say you were watching Angel?" Margie asked.

"No, no, not Angel. Angie, the little girl I've been helping for two hours. I was watching her bob that yellow umbrella up and down that I got for her off the umbrella rack."

The concerned look on Margie's face deepened. "You couldn't have gotten an umbrella for her. This rain has caused a run on umbrellas. We gave away our last one yesterday. Are you all right?" she asked, looking at me more closely. "I believe you've been crying."

"Yes, but it's not because something's wrong. It's more like I've found something that's right. It's just a little overdue Christmas spirit running over."

I turned back to look at the parking lot. It was still empty. The rain and lights really distort things, I thought to myself. She was probably closer to the side than I thought and had turned off to one side just as I turned away. That had to be it. I know she was here. She was too real not to have been. Yes, that was it. My teary eyes and everything else just played a trick on me. That explanation satisfied me. But, as I turned to go help straighten up the shelves before closing time, there was one nagging question: "Where did that yellow umbrella come from?"

13
The Last Time I Did Magic

When I was a boy I was an avid reader of most anything I could get my hands on, especially detective stories and comic books. One thing about comic books was the back cover which contained advertisements of products that every boy needed. I don't recall any directed toward girls.

Every issue of most comics featured a Charles Atlas course in bodybuilding. The ad would show a big brute of a man kicking sand in some skinny boy's face (the 97 pound weakling) at the beach and making off with his girl. Of course, the boy would send off for a Charles Atlas course and begin working out at home. The last panel would show the boy back at the beach whipping up on the bully with a whole bevy of beautiful girls casting admiring glances his way. Since we weren't near any beaches, I never considered Charles' course.

Another ad pictured a necktie which was blue with some sort of floral vine twisting its way down its length. It was pretty in the light but in the dark it became seductive with glow-in-the-dark words asking, "Will you kiss me in the dark, Baby?" The picture featured several good-looking girls swooning around a man wearing the tie on a darkened dance floor. I was sort of intrigued by this product but since I'd not yet reached puberty, I did not realize its true potential. It cost a whole dollar.

But there was one ad that really caught my fancy. For fifty cents you could get a book on how to do magic. A fellow in a top hat was pictured. He had a wand in one hand

and a bunch of fanned playing cards in the other. He was surrounded by a crowd of admiring spectators marveling at the amazing tricks he was performing. A master of these magical skills would make anyone the toast of the community.

I became fascinated with the idea of doing magic and with the promise of popularity which would be the natural result. But it would have been an exercise in futility to ask my parents for such a sum of money for what they would consider a frivolous purchase. My allowance was usually spent in town on Saturday. But the lure of stardom was too strong to resist. So I began to put a few pennies and an occasional nickel from my 25 cent per week allowance into an old sock each week. My cache grew ever so slowly. Counting it several times a week failed to increase its speed. But after an eternity or two, the magic total was reached.

The next Saturday the sock made a trip to town with me and its contents were converted into two quarters. I filled out the order form, taped the coins to a piece of cardboard, and reluctantly asked Mama for an envelope and a three-cent stamp.

"Who're you writing to?" she asked.

"Nobody," I answered. "I'm ordering something."

"What?"

"A book on how to do magic tricks."

"Did I hear you right? How much does it cost?"

"Yes 'um. Fifty-cents."

"Where'd you get fifty-cents?"

"I saved it from my allowance."

"You don't need to order any junk like that. And you sure don't need to be learning any magic." She spoke the last word as if it were something nasty.

"But, please Mama, it's my money. I saved it."

"It may be but you're not ordering anything unless I say so. And you want me to give you a stamp. Those things are expensive and not to be thrown away on junk. They'll just take your money and you won't get anything. Anyway, I need my stamps for my letters."

"Pleeese, Mama." I begged. "I'll pay you back out of my next allowance." After this and a lot more begging, she gave in and the order went into the mailbox.

The ad had said, "allow 30 days for delivery." I marked the calendar and waited. After about two weeks, I began to lay in wait every day for the mailman. Finally, after twenty-three days, a small package came with my name on it.

The little booklet was about four by six inches in size and printed on pulp paper. The print was small and hard to read and the few diagrams were fuzzy and difficult to follow. Included in the package were two or three pages of ads on magician's props—wands, top hats, scarves, balls, etc. It was then it hit me that I just had the directions with no materials to work with. And all the props were expensive—way beyond my twenty-five cent allowance. It looked as if Mama had been right.

After a few days, I hit upon a plan. I asked Mama if we had a deck of cards around the house knowing full well that we didn't. "No. What do you need with cards?" she inquired.

"I want to work on some magic card tricks," I replied. "Can we get a deck when we go to town on Saturday?"

"NO!" she said emphatically. "Cards are of the Devil and we're not having them in this house. I never should have let you get that magic book. There's no telling what you'll get into next."

She did not seem happy but I pressed on. "We've got some Rook cards," I stated.

"Rook's different."

"Does the Devil not know how to play Rook?" I asked innocently.

"Don't get smart with me young man."

"I'm sorry. Could I use the Rook cards?"

"No, you can't. You'd wear them out and then we'd have nothing to play with when the Coldwells come over.

I went back to my book to see if there were any tricks I could learn without having to buy anything. One requiring a rabbit and a hat caught my eye. I had a couple of old straw hats and I could catch a rabbit. There was plenty of scrap chicken wire around which I used to make a small pen in the corner of the yard. On the second night, my trap produced a rabbit. I was in business.

It took a good while of feeding and petting before my catch got tame enough to handle. While the taming was in progress, I was reading up on the particulars on the trick. The book was real blurry in that section and I had a hard time understanding exactly all that was involved but I finally got it down—or so I thought.

When he got so I could handle him, I got my hat and went to work. This irritated the animal no end but I was determined and kept at it. After a few days, he quit eating and would try to hide in the corner of his pen when he saw me coming. Then, one morning he was gone. He must have jumped out because there were no holes in the fence. I never knew a rabbit could jump that high. He had apparently gone to great heights to avoid a career in show business.

There was nothing to do but to get out my trap and start over. I was no more successful with the second rabbit but at least he didn't jump out of the pen. Since I had never seen a magician and only had a blurry book to go by I surmised that I wasn't doing something right.

One Saturday I ran into a boy I knew from school at the drug store. Danny lived in town so his folks had to have money and to have been places. "You ever seen a magician?" I asked.

"Sure have. Saw one last year at the State fair. He did all sorts of tricks. The best one was when he sawed the woman in half."

"Gosh!" I never heard of such a thing!" I exclaimed. "Did it kill her?"

"Naw. He put her back together."

"I don't think that one's in my book."

"What book is that?" Danny asked.

"I've got a book on magic tricks, and I'm learning how to do some of 'em. Say, did the fellow you saw do anything with a rabbit and a hat?"

"He sure did. He had a big, white rabbit."

"The one I'm using is brown. Do you think it makes any difference?"

"Naw. I don't think color would be a problem. Just what are you having trouble with?"

"Well," I answered, "my book is not very clear and I think it has left something out. I don't think I'd have much trouble getting it out if I could just get it in. And my book doesn't say which end to put the hat in."

Danny laughed so hard that he fell off the soda fountain stool and spilled his milk shake. When he finally quit laughing, he described to me what he'd seen the magician do. I was so embarrassed that I just went and sat in the car until time to go home.

And when I got home, I turned the rabbit loose and threw my magic book in the trash. And that's the last time I did magic. Not long after that certain changes began to take place and I have regretted ever since that I didn't save up for the glow-in-the-dark tie.

14
John's First Trial

"Is that where you wear them?" asked the alteration lady out of one side of her mouth. The other side was filled with several long straight pins. John wondered if she had ever swallowed any. Her disposition was such that he suspected she had one or two stuck in her craw at the moment.

"Yes . . . uh, yes, that's about right," replied John as he tugged somewhat timidly at the waistband of his new trousers.

"Well, now, I don't want any about" snorted the lady as she knelt beside the little platform on which John stood. "Get 'em exactly. When I mark these for cuffs, I want 'em to break just right in front. I don't want you to slide 'em down and walk all over 'em at the heel. And I surely don't want you pullin' 'em up and lookin' like you growed six inches last week." The way she had to talk with the pins in her mouth gave her voice an unusual tonal quality.

"Yes, that's it exactly." John hoped his voice had a more definite quality. The lady busied herself with the pant legs, using the pins and a flat piece of tailor's chalk.

John admitted to himself that the store still intimidated him. He'd never shopped in it except for socks or ties or other small items. He'd always bought his suits and jackets off the rack at cheaper places. But now here he was buying an expensive suit under the watchful eyes of his uncle.

The lady rose and walked all around John, admiring her handiwork. She ran an expert forefinger inside the waistband at the back and slid it around to one side and then the other. "I think the waist's fine. I don't think we need to mess with it any. Now, let's see about the vest and coat. I guess you left'em in the dressing room. Don't move, I'll go get 'em."

As she disappeared in the direction of the dressing rooms, John turned to his uncle, who was leaning against a nearby display case. "Uncle Arvin, I've ***never*** bought such an expensive suit. I've got a couple that look pretty good. Are you sure this is necessary?"

His uncle straightened up and moved a step or two closer. "Of course, I'm sure. Otherwise we wouldn't be doing it. If you're going to practice law with me, you're going to look the part. I don't want you in court looking like some down-at-the-heels shyster who can't afford a decent suit of clothes. Now, I don't want to hear any more about it."

The alteration lady reappeared with the vest and coat. John slipped the vest on and as he began to button it, his mind began to reflect on the course of events which had brought him to the three-by-three foot platform in Booth's Shop for Men.

He'd grown up on a farm in the southern part of the county. His parents and older brother were still there. His brother loved to farm. John didn't. Ever since he could remember he'd wanted to be a lawyer like his Uncle Arvin, his father's only brother.

"This vest's all right around the shoulders, but your waist's not very big. I'll take some out of the back here and taper it down where it'll fit good at the bottom." She began to use her chalk and pins on the back of the vest.

As he was finishing high school near the top of his class, his uncle had come to him with a proposition. Arvin had three daughters, none of whom were at all interested in law. Few girls were in 1940. John was going to have to have some financial help if he went to college. More than his parents could afford. So Arvin offered to help him with college and law school if John would agree to return and join him in his law practice. The long-range plan was for John eventually to take over the practice when Arvin retired.

"That does it for the vest. Here, slip on the coat."

Since John was in his second year of college when the United States entered World War II, he was allowed to graduate before going into the service. Arvin's membership on the local draft board helped to ensure this. After training, he was sent to Europe and arrived just as hostilities ceased. Just as he got to the Pacific, the first Bomb was dropped on Hiroshima. So, his military career consisted of a great deal of travel and no fighting.

"Did you know that your right arm is almost an inch longer than your left?" asked the alteration lady. She continued without waiting for an answer, "That's easily fixed." Her chalk did its work on the sleeves.

After his discharge, John chose Cumberland Law School for his law degree. He'd done rather well there, graduating near the top of his class. This pleased his Uncle Arvin, who knew a good investment when he saw it.

"Keep the coat buttoned. We're going to have to get some out of the back and sides here to make it fit well in the waist." Her chalk made several long marks in these areas. "OK, that hangs good. You can go slip it off now." John headed for the dressing room.

As he removed the new suit, John thought about how hard he'd studied for the bar exam and how proud Arvin had been of him for passing it on his first attempt. Now here he was, John Bowlin, Attorney at Law, being fitted for an expensive suit at Booth's in preparation for his first case. All his dreams were coming true. That explained the feeling of satisfaction that seemed to run throughout his body like an electrical current.

"How would you like to handle this?" asked the salesman as John handed him the suit. Before John could speak, Arvin spoke up, "Just bill it to him at our law office. The firm will send you a check."

The man nodded and handed John a ticket stub which said the suit could be picked up the following Tuesday.

As they left the store, John said with a note of concern in his voice, "Uncle Arvin, the firm shouldn't be buying my clothes."

"It's not," replied Arvin. "I'll just take some out of your pay for a while until it's paid for. You need the suit now and this is the quickest way to do it. Don't worry, you'll earn every thread of it before you're done. And after you get a few cases under your belt, we'll add additional suits to your wardrobe. And after a while maybe a gold watch with a fob and chain to go across the front of your vests. That really makes an impression on juries." It was obvious Arvin had big plans for his nephew.

Arvin continued, "Let's go get some lunch and then we'll go back to the office and start a breakdown on your first case." Just knowing that he was going to get to take a case to a real court sent a feeling through him that he could best describe as one of both exhilaration and trepidation at the same time. He knew that it couldn't be a big important case but it was a case, and whatever kind it was, he'd give it his best shot.

After lunch they went to Arvin's office. He handed John a file. "Most of the facts are in there. You'll want to go over all that very carefully. We are representing Odell Pinson, who is charged with a whole string of offenses—the most serious of which is attempted murder for putting a load of number 8 bird shot from a 20-gage shot gun into the rear end of his girlfriend, a Miss Hester Jean Hicks."

"Did he?" asked John.

"Well, of course he did. But the real issue here is not the act itself; it's the extenuating circumstances. That's what you've got to work on. That's what you've got to get into the record. You get enough of this before the jury and you could get an acquittal or at least a conviction on one of the lesser charges with a very light sentence and most of that suspended. Let me give you the full story and I think you'll see what I'm talking about.

"As you know, there was just a lot of economic activity started around here during the war. Probably more than this town had ever seen. The old furniture factory was converted into a war plant. It made parts for hand grenades and land mines and maybe for some other things like that. The army built Camp Frazier in the next county. A lot of the soldiers would come over here on passes looking for something to do. All this activity caused other businesses to prosper, especially eating places. The soldiers always wanted something besides army food when they would get off post.

"Help was hard to get. With most able-bodied men and some women in service and a lot of folks working in the war plant, there was a real labor shortage. This demand brought in a good number of country folks. If they could be spared on the farms, they came to town for the jobs. They could make a lot more money working in town than they could scratching around raising corn and tobacco. In a few instances, whole families sold their livestock, boarded up their houses, moved to town, and all got jobs.

"Hester Jean Hicks was one of these migrants. She came from somewhere out in the sticks around Shaggy Ridge. She got a job as a waitress in one of the new cafes on Highway 41 east of town. Roscoe Watson had set up three or four small trailers in his back yard to rent out and Hester rented one of these. With the pay and tips, she was making more money than she'd ever seen before.

"Hester's not bad looking for a country girl, and she soon discovered that there was much more money to be made entertaining the soldiers from Camp Frazier if you know what I mean.

"Now, Hester was quite enterprising. She would use her waitressing to make contacts for her second career. Her shift started at about noon and she worked until the cafe closed at eight. During her shift she would set up dates for the evening. Pretty efficient.

"The only thing that Hester had to be careful about was her boyfriend. They had found each other soon after she moved to town. Odell had come in from another county to work in the war plant. He was very jealous, but he worked the night shift six nights a week and, of course, Hester knew his schedule. She was careful not to do any entertaining on nights he was off, and she was also careful not to entertain any of the local boys who might tell Odell what she was doing. As best we can tell, she limited her second career strictly to the soldiers from Camp Frazier. You know, she was pretty smart for a country girl.

"Well, things went along pretty good for several months, but you know what they say: ''The best laid plans of mice and men sometimes get all screwed up,' or something like that. Anyway, one night everything hit the fan. Hester had made several dates for the evening and was in the process of filling them. Unbeknownst to her, there was a breakdown of some sort at the war plant and they had to shut it down early and send the workers home. This set the stage for a disaster, and sure enough, it happened.

"Odell decided to go by and see Hester on his way home. You can imagine his surprise when he rolled up to her trailer in his pickup and found two soldiers standing outside waiting their turn. When he jumped out of the truck, they took off running through the back wood lot. Odell dived back into his truck to get his shotgun, but they were gone before he could get it out and loaded.

"Hester had heard the truck come up and looked out the window and saw what was transpiring. She communicated the dire straits to the soldier in her bed. He grabbed up as much of his uniform as he could find and bolted out the only door just as Odell was getting the shells into his gun. He disappeared over the side fence, dropping his cap, one shoe, and a couple of other odd pieces of uniform before Odell was ready to fire. Hester came out buck-naked and took off down the driveway. Odell cut down on her and caught her with a full load of birdshot square in the butt. She began screaming like a wounded wildcat and dived over into some holly bushes, which did a pretty good job of scratching her up all over. The discharge of the gun and Hester's screams apparently brought Odell to his senses. He didn't shoot any more and later said he thought he'd killed her.

"All the running, screaming, and shooting soon attracted a crowd. The sheriff came and arrested Odell. Someone put a blanket around Hester and took her to the emergency room. Said it took them over two hours to pick all the birdshot out of her butt. I think all the basic facts are in that file."

"But, Uncle Arvin, everyone knows Odell did the shooting. I don't see how in the world we can find enough circumstances to cause a jury to say he's not guilty."

"My boy, what you've got to understand is that guilt or innocence doesn't even enter into the picture. You see, Odell was justified in doing what he did. Our, or rather, your job is to convince them of that. The focus of the trial must be taken off Odell and put where it belongs--on Hester. You see, she was engaged in an unmoral and illegal act. In fact, she was caught in the midst of that very act."

John interrupted, "It seems that I remember a Bible story about a woman caught in a similar situation. If I'd paid better attention in Sunday School, I could probably remember the details."

"Well, maybe so, but I don't think the Bible will help us any on this case. What you've got to do is find enough witnesses that can establish what Hester was doing on a regular basis. Also, you need to play down the seriousness of her injuries. And you've got to make the jury see that Odell just reacted normally and rightly to finding his girlfriend engaged in a despicable, immoral, illegal act. In fact, the jury can be made to see that what Hester got was deserved and that Odell was merely an instrument of righteous punishment. That's the direction you need to take."

"I'm sure you're right, Uncle Arvin."

"I know I'm right. This case will be easy to turn in that direction. And it'll be even easier when you get Hester on cross-examination. The DA will have to put her on the stand where she will be ripe for you to pick. Now, you'd better start lining up those witnesses."

John did as his uncle had directed. With a little work, he had no trouble finding several soldiers who had been to Hester's trailer on several occasions with a number of other soldiers. He had them all issued a summons so that he'd know they would show up. He also went over the sheriff's reports and the medical reports with a fine-toothed comb. He wrote out and rehearsed every possible question he could think of to ask Hester, as well as questions to come back with depending on how she answered. John was not going to be caught unprepared his first time in court. He was ready over a week before the date for the trial.

It seemed to John that the trial date took forever to arrive, but it finally did. He put on his new suit and met his uncle and Odell at the law office. As John had directed, Odell was dressed in a coat and tie, had a fresh haircut, and had pried most of the dirt out from under his fingernails. They went over a few last minute items and walked over to the courthouse.

Things went smoothly and a jury was seated and opening arguments presented before the recess for lunch. At lunch Arvin commented, "The only thing I don't like so far is that we got four women on the jury. I'd like not to have any, but I guess we did about as good as we could have done considering the choices we had. The trouble is these women think now that they can do anything a man can do. I guess the war helped that kind of thinking along. I don't know what the country's coming to."

After lunch everything moved along very predictably—at least in the beginning. The District Attorney called the sheriff, a deputy, and a couple of other people who were present to establish the facts of the case. The medical report was then introduced into evidence and the doctor who treated Hester testified as to the extent of her injuries. John had few questions for most of them, but he did get the doctor to admit that Hester's injuries were superficial and not life threatening.

Then, the time came that John had been waiting for. The prosecution called Hester to the stand. The District Attorney's aim was to establish the fact that Odell fired the shot, since Hester and Odell were the only ones present when it happened, and to establish just how painful and debilitating Hester's injuries were. He very carefully avoided any references to what had been taking place just prior to the shooting.

When the District Attorney turned to the defense table and said, "Your witness," John rose and moved slowly toward the witness stand. On the way he pulled back his coat and hooked his thumbs into the pockets of is new vest. He stood looking at Hester for several seconds before asking his first question. "Miss Hicks, you testified that you were running down Mr. Roscoe Watson's driveway to get away from my client, Mr. Odell Pinson. Others have testified that you had no clothes on. Would you please tell the court just what you were doing that caused you to be unclothed and why you were fearful of Mr. Pinson?"

The District Attorney immediately objected on the grounds that it was irrelevant and that this area had not been broached during direct examination. John was quick to point out that Mr. Pinson had been a model citizen of the community for some time and that he was not prone to taking pot-shots at folks running down driveways whether they had any clothes on or not, and that the question went to motive—what events had caused Mr. Pinson to act so out of character. The judge overruled the objection and John got Hester to admit what she had been doing that night. He intended to nail that door shut with his witnesses who would testify that she had been engaged in the world's oldest profession for several months.

Hester had not expected this turn of events. Her face was beginning to flush and she was becoming visibly agitated.

John next turned to her injuries. He recalled the doctor's statement that her injuries were "superficial and not life threatening." Hester was becoming more worked up.

Then, John asked the question that drove Hester over the edge. "Miss Hicks, it has been established that you and Mr. Pinson were at least forty yards apart at the time the shot was fired. We all know that a 20-gage shot gun is not a powerful or long-range weapon and that number 8 bird-shot are not very large. Now, Miss Hicks, you really were not injured that badly, were you?"

Hester just couldn't take any more. During John's last question, she had begun to sob and when he finished with it, she sprang into action. Before anyone knew what was happening, she jumped straight up out of the witness chair and shouted, "I wuz too hurt bad! Why, I couldn't work for near a month. And Odell Pinson, don't you just set there. Lookit what you done to me!" With that, she whirled around placing her back to the courtroom, and with one motion, bent over at the waist and flipped her full skirt up over her back,

A loud gasp came from the packed courtroom. Hester had nothing on under the skirt and as she assumed a position that would be made famous years later by Hugh Heffner and Larry Flynt, she took everybody's picture with both sets of lenses. And on both buttocks and upper thighs were the small, red dot scars showing the exact pattern of Odell's shotgun. Some local hunter remarked later that Odell's gun shot an unusually tight pattern at that range.

The gasp was followed by pandemonium. Women screamed and tried to shield the sight from their menfolk. The men jumped up on the benches to get a better view. John stood frozen in position, one thumb locked deeply into one of his vest pockets. He had been very close to Hester, and while asking his last question, had been leaning toward her to drive his point home. Her abrupt change of position had left him looking not into her face but into her ample rear. He had a close and unobstructed view of what many of the male spectators were climbing upon the benches to see.

The judge banged his gavel so hard that the head flew off and ricocheted off the defense table and into the spectators.

After what seemed like an eternity, someone got Hester covered up and back in the witness chair. The judge got the courtroom calmed down. John was so shaken that he asked for, and received, a thirty-minute recess.

After the recess John tried to carry on, but it was obvious he'd lost his edge. Even though his witnesses made some telling points and Odell did well on the stand, Hester's unconventional actions had already determined the outcome. She garnered so much sympathy from both men and women that the jury only deliberated for a little more than thirty minutes before finding Odell guilty of all charges except attempted murder.

John was the last to leave. He hid out in one of the witness rooms in the back until everyone left. He wasn't up to facing anyone. The summer sun was low in the sky before he ventured outside. He walked slowly back to his office feeling like a total failure and wondering if he had any future in the legal profession.

His new suit looked as bad as he felt. It was rumpled and wilted. The heat in the courtroom coupled with his emotional state after Hester's exposure had caused him to perspire profusely. He had sweated completely through the back and the armpits of the coat and had the rest of the suit so damp that it had completely lost its shape.

Arvin was still at the office. John found him sitting in one of the side chairs in his office staring into space. "I'm sorry, Uncle Arvin. I don't know how I messed things up so completely. Maybe I'm not cut out to be a lawyer."

Arvin looked at John for several seconds before speaking. "No, my boy, don't blame yourself. You did exactly what I told you to do and you did it well. The fault's mine for not giving you better directions and for not listening to you. You remember when we were first discussing this case and I was going on about Hester getting caught in an illegal, immoral act and you mentioned that it reminded you of a Bible story, and I just dismissed that out of hand. Well, I should have checked that out early in our preparation. After court was over this afternoon for some reason your statement began to bother me. I came over here and scratched around in my Bible until I found it. It's in the eighth chapter of John and is about the woman brought to Jesus after being caught in the very act of adultery. If I'd read it earlier, I would have known if it didn't work for the Pharisees, it surely wouldn't work for us."

15
P. G.

I was proud to count myself among P.G.'s friends. He had a lot of them. This was evident by the room full of flowers and the hundreds of people who came to mourn his passing. It hardly seems possible that he's been gone a little over a year now. I still miss him. He was one of those real people that the world has too few of. I think there ought to be some cosmic law that prohibits death from claiming people like P.G. until the world is provided with a similar replacement.

But, the purpose of this is not to dwell on his death; it is to remember his life--the kind of person he was and some of the things he stood for.

P.G.'s main job

P.G.'s main job was with the U. S. Government, but he lived on a farm on which he raised cattle and hay for feed. During the haying season he would hire a number of high school-aged boys to help with the operation. The baling of the rectangular bales took a good bit of labor.

P.G. had served in France during World War II and had lost a foot and a part of his lower leg in the struggle. He wore an artificial foot and walked so well on it that it was hard to tell it wasn't the real item.

P.G. loved to tell stories, play jokes, laugh, and have a good time. He had one joke he liked to pull in the hay field with his artificial leg. Any new boy who didn't know about his leg was fair game. The leg and foot were made of wood which looked like mahogany. It had several holes through it, probably to cut down on the weight. The bales were handled with hay hooks, iron hooks with a "T" handle. P.G. would take a hay hook, work it through his sock, through a hole in the leg, then through the sock on the opposite side. He would then proceed to fall out on the ground holding his leg a few inches above the penetration and issuing loud cries of pain. Everyone would come running to see what the problem was.

To the uninitiated, it appeared that P.G. had impaled his leg with the hay hook. The veteran workers who knew what was happening would add to the seriousness of the situation with anguished cries of their own and comments like "Never seen one that bad," "They'll probably have to cut his leg off," "If it's got an artery, he'll die before we can get him to town."

During all this commotion, P.G. would be imploring the

new boy, "Help me, son! Pull it out!" Usually he could get the boy to do just that, which would effect an amazing recovery. P.G. would immediately return to normal, get up, and say, "OK, let's get back to work." Seeing no blood on the hook he was holding, as well as seeing the rest of the boys convulsed with laughter, the new boy would realize that he'd been the butt of a very good practical joke. Of course, the next time there was a new hand in the field, he would get to participate along with the other initiated ones.

A Child's Instruction

P.G., along with his wife, Ruth, raised and educated three fine sons. I was privileged to teach two of them. They are now all successful, respected adults who reflect the principles and values which were so much a part of P.G.'s life. P.G. was not one to mince words. He called things as he saw them and apologized to no one for the principles he believed in--things like honesty, responsibility, dependability, helpfulness, concern for others, to name only a few.

His main job was with the U. S. Department of Agriculture, where he worked with a number of veterinarians. He got to share one of his basic philosophies of child-rearing one day with one of them.

This particular doctor had a teenage son with whom he was having a lot of problems. The boy would not come in at his curfew time, he had wrecked two or three cars, and he was heavily involved with drugs. For several days running, as they worked, his problem with his son was the doctor's main topic of conversation. He went over the litany of things he couldn't get the boy to do, as well as the things he was doing wrong. P.G. made little response, until one day the doctor said, "I just don't know what I'm going to do. He's 16. He's too big to whip."

P.G. stood up, looked him in the eye, and replied, "Doc, he ain't always been 16, has he?" The doctor just dropped his head and walked away as P.G.'s arrow hit home. P.G. believed in starting a child's instruction in the cradle and working up from there. It's hard to argue with that policy, since he got such good results with it.

Health Problems

As he grew older, P.G. had a number of health problems. His heart was the first major organ to fail. After a couple of close calls, his doctors recommended bypass surgery as the only solution. We were all concerned, but not just about the operation itself. We had heard or known of people who had undergone significant personality changes after this type of surgery. They had gone from being pleasant, wonderful people to being cranky, suspicious, and hard to get along with. We prayed that it would not have a similar effect on P.G. He was such a great person to talk to, to travel with, or just be around that we could not imagine him any other way. We need not have worried. Before he left the hospital, P.G. knew all the nurses and orderlies on his wing. They would come by to visit with him at slack times, and he became a bright spot in their lives even though he was the one flat on his back with a scar from his throat to his navel. In fact and to his credit even as his health deteriorated, never did he lose any of his good-natured humor or zest for living. Even while sick, P.G. was a better man than most.

Pretty soon after the doctors got the plumbing in his heart all fixed up, they found an irregularity in his lower colon. It was cancer. The surgeons snipped out that section and spliced the remaining intestine back together. They couldn't find any more and were reasonably sure they'd gotten it all. They were wrong. In a few years the cancer came back more widespread than before. This time the surgeons had to snip out much more of the intestine. In fact, when they got through, they did not have enough of the good parts left to reach the exit. So, they made a new exit in his side to which they attached a bag to catch the waste. P.G.

now had a reworked heart and a colostomy.

About a week after this surgery, I went to visit him in the hospital. He related an incident that had just occurred. It seems that . . . but let him tell the story.

"You know, Luke, I guess they don't even know whether or not one of these things is going to work until it does. Before they cut on me, they wouldn't let me have anything but liquids. This cleaned the solid stuff out of me pretty good. After the cuttin' they started letting me have some solid food. The nurses were checking that bag five or six times a day. That morning nurse seemed real concerned that nothing was coming through. Well, you wouldn't believe what happened yesterday morning. That nurse came in and found something in the bag. She got so excited she was almost beside herself. She went running off down the hall and got another nurse and made her come and look at it. Then, she went back out in the hall and got two orderlies and had them look. About that time, one of the doctors came in to see what all the commotion was about and he got to see it. Nothing would do but he had to go out and get one of his doctor buddies to come and take a look. I'm telling you one thing, Luke, I've never seen so many people get so worked up over a handful of shit."

P.G. was truly a practitioner of the Biblical admonition not to think of yourself more highly than you ought to think. He didn't think he was particularly special. But for us who knew him and were influenced by him, we know that he was.

As I reflect on P.G. and the way he lived his life, there comes to mind one of the ultimate compliments which could be paid to a person by settlers of the Old West. It was, "He'll do to ride the river with." In that day, much travel was done on rivers in two-man boats. In rough waters and especially in rapids, the man in the bow had to have confidence in the man in the stern and vice-versa. He had to be a person of steady nerve, good judgment, courage, strength, and dependability. In other words, the other man in the boat had to be the type of person you could trust in any situation, up to, and including, life or death. Yes, P.G. was the kind of man you could ride the river with.

16
The Judgment

Old Sam was dead.

His death was not a recent event. But last Saturday's auction had brought back the memory of his passing. On that day beginning at ten o'clock, Sam's house and all his worldly possessions were sold to the highest and sometimes only bidders.

He had only two heirs, nephews who lived a long way off. But heirs didn't matter. Sam's property fetched only a little more than enough to pay his debts and funeral expenses.

By noon, all Sam's furniture and meager possessions had been carted away. The house was just before falling totally down. Portions of it had already succumbed to decay and gravity. It was bought by his neighbor, who intended to demolish it and extend his yard and "beautify" the street.

In a few weeks, the small tombstone in Willow Mount Cemetery would be the only physical evidence of Sam Bradley's existence. He had lived for 78 years in this small Tennessee town, and would be reduced to a few letters and numerals on a small block of granite.

It was Monday morning after the auction. I had stopped by Dock Arnold's shop to pass the time of day. I was not a native of the town. That is to say, I had not been born there and would, therefore, always be an outsider. However, through seven years of residence and genuine effort, I had made the "tolerated" category. The townsfolk were civil to me and allowed a certain degree of association, but it was evident that a greater intimacy was out of the question.

Dock was the town handyman, and his shop reflected that calling. The title "shop" was rather pretentious, but since it was Dock's personal designation, the townspeople went along with his wishes. The building was really an old, one-car garage--one of those which had been built fifty years after the completion of the main house when the family purchased their first automobile. It was of clapboard construction with a tin roof and a dirt floor. Its location about sixty yards from the residence had insured its survival when the house caught fire.

The large, hand-hewn foundation stones, parts of two chimneys, and the front steps were the only evidence that a stately building once occupied that site. The limestone steps were now a stairway which led only to the large walnut tree growing inside the foundation. The fire had also taken all the nearby outbuildings, leaving the garage as a lone sentinel in the corner of the lot near the street.

The owners collected a small amount of rent and allowed Dock to treat the garage pretty much as his own. He had it wired for electricity and built a shed porch on the front where he could usually be found—weather permitting—working on a piece of furniture. He was a master at replacing broken chair rungs, weaving chair bottoms, making cabinet doors, and performing hundreds of other cures for old furniture.

The building leaned precariously to the west in a Tennessee imitation of Pisa's famous structure. A few years earlier, after the tilt had increased to the point that it seemed to defy the law of gravity, Dock went to the local sawmill and got three cedar poles with bark still intact. With these propped against its side, the garage ceased its migration toward the horizontal. It also gave Dock's shop the distinction of being the only building in town with flying buttresses.

That Monday, Dock was sitting under the porch shed working on a rocking chair. I sat down on one of the empty nail kegs that served as seats for his frequent visitors. Dock was one craftsman who did not allow working to get in the way of visiting. Of course, he rarely stopped his activities when anyone dropped by. This was especially true of the town loafers, who made the shop one of their afternoon stations on their daily circuit of the town's loafing places. Dock was a true master of the art of visiting and working at the same time.

We exchanged pleasantries about the summer heat, the lack of rain, and each other's health. Dock continued his effort on the chair. It was an old oak rocker, well made and sturdy. He was obviously going to restore it since he was in the process of removing the old finish. It would be a beautiful piece after Dock worked his magic on it.

"That's a nice looking chair you've got there, Dock."

"Yep. Hit's old Sam's chair. Bought it las' Sa'day." Dock paused, but his scraper continued its work. I made no reply, for I knew that his observations were not complete. When he got started on a subject, he would eventually say all that he was going to say if his listener just let him go at his own measured pace. There would often be long moments of silence while he sanded on some chair part or applied a coat of varnish to a cabinet. At times it would appear that he lost all contact with the topic; but just then, he would resume his laconic discourse. I had learned a great deal over the years about the community and its people by just sitting on one of Dock's nail kegs and listening. In fact, it was from Dock that I had learned that old Sam Bradley had spent his early years chasing women and drinking. Eventually, he seemed to grow tired of the chasing and spent his last twenty years or so concentrating on the drinking.

Questions or attempts to steer Dock's monologue would cause him to clam up. One simply had to sit patiently to see just how much information he was willing to divulge. It was maddening at times, but a small trickle was better than no water at all.

The chair was covered with several layers of brown paint. Dock was scraping on one of the arms where the paint had softened through time and contact with body oils and sweat. The paint came up in waxy brown curls ahead of the scraper.

"And this here's som'a old Sam's grease."

Scrape . . . scrape . . . scrape.

Dock shifted his chaw of Brown Mule to the other jaw and shot a stream of tobacco juice into a nearby pile of wood shavings.

"Yep. He's dead an' in Hell, I guess."

Scrape . . . scrape.

The scraper stopped abruptly as it seemed to dawn on Dock the fate he had pronounced on old Sam. The chair was forgotten for the moment as Dock leaned back with his eyes looking across the street at nothing in particular. Unconsciously, he wiped the scraper on his pant leg. His tongue rolled the wad of tobacco around his mouth. He seemed to be groping for something--a philosophical truth which would support his pronouncement—a truth that he could feel, but had trouble putting into words with his limited command of formal English. The inner struggle continued for two or three minutes.

Then his eyes came back into focus, the tobacco ceased its journey, and the scraper again peeled the brown curls off the chair arm. Dock had managed to get his feelings and words into juxtaposition.

"Yep, dead and in Hell."

Scrape . . . scrape . . . scrape.

"Iffen he ain't . . . there ain't no use in havin' one."

17
Some Never Give Up

It was Thursday afternoon and head nurse Edwina Craul was in her cubbyhole office catching up on some of her records when she was interrupted by a series of loud thumps accompanied by an equally loud string of oaths. She rushed out to find Dub and Sam, two of the custodians, trying to move a large piece of furniture down to Wing-B. The commotion had attracted the attention of the patients in the sun room who were craning their necks or moving their wheelchairs for a better view of the excitement. The oaths were coming from Dub who fell silent when Edwina's door burst open.

With so many eyes focused on them, Edwina resolved not to raise her voice. Through clenched teeth she said, "You boys knock off all this racket and cussing and get that thing down to B-7."

"Yes 'um," replied Sam as he dropped his head and looked at the floor.

Dub was not so compliant. "Well, we wouldn't be making no noise effen y'all 'ud put some limit on the size of this stuff these old folks bring in here. What do they need with all their furniture anyway? We got to move this in and the old woman won't live six months and we'll jest have to move it out again. They's jest comin' here to die, thas' all."

Edwina was livid. "Come in my office, Dub," she commanded. He did so with a little swagger in his step. Sam stood outside shuffling his weight from one foot to the other. The patients continued to maneuver for better vantage points.

After a few minutes, Dub emerged with all the starch taken out of him. Edwina had explained the facts of life and the facts of his employment in words he had no trouble understanding. Without a word Dub took hold of one side of the breakfront. Sam hastily grabbed the other and they headed toward B-7, puffing loudly but uttering no other sounds. Edwina went back into her office; the patients settled back to their former positions.

Edwina sat mulling over what Dub had said. She was sorry the patients had heard him. She hated to admit that he was right. They were all just here to find a place to die. Her job was to make them as comfortable as possible during their last days. She considered it her calling and if a few things from home would help to make them more content, so be it. Dub would just have to move them or find someplace else to work.

The next day Mrs. Zerphylia Ousley's son, Merlin, came by to set up her room. He brought several boxes with him. Edwina had met him when he had made the arrangements. She dropped by B-7 and found him arranging the contents of the boxes in the breakfront. It was not an especially fine piece—not mahogany or cherry or walnut. Edwina guessed it was poplar with some dark, reddish finish which was shrinking and cracking in places and peeling off in others. Some of the knobs were missing, a lower door hung crooked on a loose hinge, and one of the top doors had a cracked glass.

After an exchange of pleasantries, Merlin continued to put things away while talking about his mother. Edwina did not interrupt.

"Until my company transferred me back here, I didn't realize how bad Mother had gotten. So much change just in the last year—all for the worse. Can't take care of herself anymore. Doesn't know where she is half the time. I know it's a matter of time, so I'm going to try to make it the best I can for her. She'll feel better with some of her stuff around her. And I'm gonna come by every day I'm in town to try to give her a little happiness. She deserves that from me. You know, she has not had a happy life with Dad being an alcoholic and abusing us the way he did. And no matter how bad she gets, I'm not gonna quit. I'll bring her in this weekend."

Merlin hardly seemed to notice when Edwina excused herself.

The first thing Edwina noted about Mrs. Ousley was the symptoms of Alzheimer's, especially the blank, vacant eyes which only infrequently emitted a spark of lucidness. She'd seen so many. Maybe six months to a year.

Edwina always made it a point to give some special attention to new patients but for the first week of Mrs. Ousley's stay, she had to spend a lot of time dealing with "the great escape."

Miss Mattie Lou and Miss Jessie were sisters. Their rooms were in different wings. Miss Jessie could still walk and could find Miss Mattie Lou's room. She would come for a visit every day and push Miss Mattie Lou around the halls in her wheelchair. They were like two young girls playing together. They usually took their afternoon naps together in Miss Mattie Lou's bed.

One day they decided that they hadn't seen Mama in a long time so it was time to go for a visit. Of course, Mama had been dead over forty years and the nursing home was in another town at least thirty miles from where they had lived. Since none of this really registered with them, they were not to be deterred. They got a paper sack and packed a few items they would need for the journey and concealed it under Miss Mattie Lou's lap robe. They got out a rear door without being seen but were apprehended as they crossed the courtyard headed for the woods.

Of course, the families had to be notified and Miss Mattie Lou's room had to be moved so that Miss Jessie could no longer locate it. It was a shame since they enjoyed each other's company so much but there was no telling what they might try next. And Edwina did not have enough staff to watch them all the time.

What was it with some of these old people Edwina wondered. They kept on scratching and clawing and holding on to things and clinging to life when death would be the best answer. There had to be something tenacious in the human spirit. Edwina had seen it too many times to think otherwise.

Even in dealing with "the great escape," Edwina noted that Merlin did come every day. And as she passed B-7 she could see him holding some item that he had taken out of the breakfront and talking about a happy event connected with it. One day it was a lace tablecloth as Merlin talked about the family members who once sat around it. Another, it was a large platter with him describing the turkeys she used to fix for holidays. Sometime Mrs. Ousley even laughed. And Edwina noticed that there was a sparkle in her eye and a set to her jaw she had not seen earlier.

One morning Edwina stopped by B-7 for a visit. Mrs. Ousley seemed pleased. They talked about the meals and the bingo game scheduled for that afternoon. Then Edwina asked, "Will your son be by today?"

"Yes, but it'll be late in the afternoon."

"I notice he comes almost every day."

"Yes, he's good to me. Got a good job, too."

"You must be very proud of him."

"I am. I am. He's made something of himself in spite of everything."

Mrs. Ousley's last statement puzzled Edwina but she continued. "I've seen him talking with you about your things, about happy times, with the tablecloth and platter and other things."

Mrs. Ousley did not respond immediately. She sat staring out the window for so long that Edwina thought her mind must have gone elsewhere. But such was not the case. Finally, her gaze turned back to Edwina.

"Yes, Merlin likes to remember the pleasant things. He didn't unfold the tablecloth so that you could see the burned place on one end. That happened when Big Merlin came in drunk one Thanksgiving. Messed up the tablecloth and knocked over the candle stand. Took the turkey off the platter and threw it out in the yard. Then he beat both of us. That was the worst part. No, Merlin's not had a happy life. I'm glad he's coming by so I can help him with some pleasant memories. I know I don't have much time left but

I'm gonna use it to give him some happiness. Mamas have to do that, you know. It must be our nature."

18
Doc Kennon

While an undergraduate at Ole Miss in the early 1950s, I found myself in need of a science course to complete that requirement. Some of my friends on the football team advised me to sign up for a beginning astronomy course. Since they prided themselves on being able to locate the easiest courses in any department, I listened to them.

They said the course was taught by "Old Doc Kennon," who was so old that he didn't know what was going on. According to them, you had to go to class and get counted present, but then you could slip out. Also, the class was so easy that you could borrow someone's notes and read them over a coupla times along with reading a little in the textbook and make a "C" with hardly any effort. Astronomy 1A sounded like just what I needed, a class I could pull a "C" in with little study and no class attendance. So, I signed up for it. However, I soon discovered that things were not going to work out exactly as I had planned.

The class met in one of the large lecture rooms in the physical science building. It was a tiered room with permanent desks bolted to the floor. I estimated that it would hold about a hundred students. The only student entrance was through a set of double swinging doors situated at the back of the right side as one faced the front.

There were seating charts posted on the door and around the room. A rather elderly man stood at the front with his arms folded, leaning back against one of the demo tables. He didn't say anything, but just waited for us to figure out the charts and find our assigned seats. He wore a rumpled suit which still bore the remains of chalk dust from the previous semester. The knot of his tie was hidden under one of the collar points and the tie itself did not lie flat on the shirt front, but hung facing the left as if the wearer had suddenly made a quick turn without the tie following suit. He had tousled white hair, watery eyes, and a rather rubbery face. He viewed the seat search through, and at times, over eyeglasses which were perched toward the end of his nose. His lower lip bobbed up and down against the upper, keeping time to some private rhythm. I assumed that he was "old Doc Kennon." I was right.

I was dismayed when I found my seat. Since my name began with a "B," I got to sit on the front row, and since the chart started on the left as one faced the front, I got a seat that was just about as far from the doors in the right rear as one could get. Right then I kissed the idea of slipping out good-bye. Too much distance. I was stuck in Astronomy 1A with no prospects of escape. What a revolting turn this was.

No one slipped out that first day, because Doc Kennon stood looking at the class as he gave us the course requirements and syllabus and covered all the general housekeeping items. Anyway, he didn't keep us the whole period.

On the second day, Doc Kennon took the roll by marking the empty seats on his seating chart. This done, he turned to the blackboard and began to illustrate some principle of astronomy. As he talked, the exodus began and was fascinating to watch.

My seat placement allowed me to observe Doc Kennon

and the goings on in the rest of the room at the same time. Since there was only one exit, all those leaving had to funnel themselves toward the right rear. It also meant that those near the door had to leave first, so that those pressing behind would have empty seats in which to seek refuge when Doc Kennon turned to face the class. The effect was very similar to waves breaking on a seashore. As soon as one wave of students would break through the door, another wave would flow into their vacated seats and others into theirs and so on. Then, another would break out to freedom and the process would be repeated until the only ones left were the serious students and pockets of us unfortunates trapped because of location. On a normal day, there would be twenty to thirty students left after twenty minutes or so.

The ebb and flow of the whole class was interesting, but equally fascinating was the individual styles of departure. Some were very adept at the "360 degree spin." They would grab the chair arm, roll out in a clockwise turn to the right, and come to rest in the next seat. The good ones could move up to three spaces this way; however, excessive use of the maneuver could make one dizzy and put the body out of control. Also, because the back was turned to the front for half of the spin, it was not good for long distances.

Some just stood up and walked while keeping an eye on Doc Kennon. If he started to turn around, they would drop into a vacant seat and wait. Those caught between empty seats would kneel in among the seated students until the opportunity to move again presented itself. This could be awkward if one had to remain in this position for very long.

The more cautious would not leave one seat unless they knew their next stop. They tended to dart around in a crouched position among the rows of seats and walking students throwing furtive glances in all directions. I thought they would make good infantrymen since they already had the basic moves down. I could picture them in combat dress armed with M-1 rifles attacking "Pork Chop Hill" or some other Communist Chinese stronghold in Korea.

As I noted, I was seated where I had a good view of Doc Kennon. Although some of his movements were rather slow, his eyes were sharp and alert and there was surely nothing wrong with his mind. When he turned to face the class, he always did so in a very measured way, not unlike a boxer telegraphing a right-hand lead. He usually did not turn until the noise level from students moving on the creaking hardwood floors reached a level over which he could not be heard. At that point the chalk would go into the tray and his body would begin a shuffling rotation to the front. Those in migration at that moment would locate seats or kneeling places, and all would be quiet and in order when he finally got completely turned. He would survey the class over his glasses, his lower lip would bob up and down against the upper a few times, he would clear his throat a couple of times, and continue his lecture. It might be several minutes before he turned to the board to illustrate another point. It did not take many days before I realized that "old Doc Kennon" knew exactly what was going on. I tried to tell that to some of my friends, but they would not believe me. But I knew better. It was like watching an old grizzled tomcat playing with a bunch of mice who'd been caught and didn't realize it.

The only time I recall him turning around quickly was the day the dogs got roused up. It was one of those cold, sunny days in winter. Five or six of the campus dogs had gotten into the lobby of the building and had found a good warm place to sleep where the sun streamed through the lobby windows and heated an area of the dark floor. Unfortunately, this place was just outside the swinging doors of our classroom. Doc Kennon was turned to the board, and about half the class was in motion. The first two or three out the doors were looking back to see that he wasn't turned round to see them, and didn't see the sleeping canines. They tripped and fell in amongst the animals which caused all hell to break loose. Startled from their slumber, the dogs immediately reverted to pre-domesticated reactions. They began barking, howling, snarling, and biting each other and any students who happened to be close enough. The din did not begin at a low level and increase in volume. It started at the crescendo and stayed there for several minutes. It seemed to freeze those in the classroom in space and time. Doc Kennon whirled around with a speed no one thought he possessed to see twenty or so of his class on their feet and frozen in position. The swinging doors were going back and forth, revealing glimpses of the melee going on in the lobby. Doc Kennon assessed the situation quickly. His lower lip smacked the upper a few times. He cleared his throat, "Hrumph, hrumph," and commented, "Those dogs seem to be really stirred up today." Then, as things calmed down in the lobby, he turned back to his illustration at the board and everything returned to normal.

My football team friends began to tease me about not slipping out of the class. Even after I pointed out to them the location of my seat, they wouldn't let up. Said anyone could slip out on old Doc Kennon. So, I resolved to give it a try.

I had to wait for a good bit of the room to clear and I had to be extra careful since I had to pass within a few feet of his lecture table. I managed to work my way over to the center aisle, but found that it was not easy going up the tiers backwards. After many short periods of movement and several long periods of waiting, I managed to slip through the swinging doors. It was a nerve-wracking experience. I checked my watch. The class was fifty minutes long; I had exited at the forty-two minute mark. All that trouble for eight minutes? I marked that up as a poor return for the investment and resolved to stay in class and take my chances. Anyway, I was beginning to find the class and Doc Kennon kind of interesting.

As the days passed, those leaving increased, which meant that the movement and noise during class increased proportionately. But Doc Kennon had a way of slowing down the departures.

He always had a clipboard with a clean, class seating chart. With the ringing of the last bell, he would dutifully date the chart, mark it, and place it on the corner of his lecture table. On this particular day, the class began just that way, but, with about five minutes left in the period, he looked at his chart and said with a touch of exasperation at himself in his voice, "Oh my goodness, class. I've forgotten to take the roll. Just let me do that before the bell." As he picked up his clipboard, someone raised his hand and said, "Doctor Kennon, I believe you took the roll at the start of class." Doc Kennon looked at the clipboard and then turned up a pristine chart for all to see. "No," he replied, "I always mark a seating chart and, as you can see, this one hasn't been marked yet. I guess I'm just getting forgetful." With that, he took the real roll, looking over his glasses with that lower lip working and going, "Tsk, tsk, tsk. A lot of absentees today. Wonder where they could be. Maybe there's something happening on campus that I'm unaware of."

I looked at a few of the others around the front. They were having as hard a time as I was keeping from laughing out loud. We never figured out how or when he got that fresh chart on the clipboard. When the word got around to those who had left, many were quite angry and blamed the class cut they got on "that senile old professor who couldn't even remember taking roll." They wouldn't even listen when some of us tried to tell them differently. Yes, old Doc Kennon had us all by the short hairs. There were some who were just too dumb to realize it. At any event, his immediate purpose was accomplished. Attendance for the whole class period improved markedly from that point, resulting in much less movement and noise.

Doc Kennon gave several tests during the semester. The first was scheduled about two weeks before the final course drop date. Any course could be dropped before that date without penalty. Afterwards there had to be a grade with the drop.

All of Doc Kennon's tests were multiple choice. He told us before the first one that he was being very generous with his grading. He said, "Why, statistics will show that you can come in here and not know anything about any question, guess at all of them, and still make a raw score of 14."

He got the results back to us promptly. I did pretty well on it. One of my football team friends who could always pick the crip courses said to me on the way out after class.

"Luke, you may be right about old Doc Kennon. He said we could guess on all of them and still get a raw score of 14. Well, I did and I got a 14. I think I'll stop by after lunch and drop before I get an 'F' on my record."

Apparently, a number of other class members used the same reasoning. At the next class meeting, Doc Kennon walked in with a handful of drop slips and proceeded to take them off his chart. The class was reduced by about 40 percent. At that point, the strategic date placement of the first test dawned on me. Doc Kennon had suffered a number of fools with much patience for a few weeks, but then he effectively reduced his class to those who were going to stay in class and do at least a moderate amount of study for the rest of the semester. And some still saw him as a bumbling old man? He did seem to go out of his way to cultivate that image, but he'd always been in control and I suspected that he would remain so. I would not have tried to match wits with him on a bet.

The class seemed to get more interesting after the mass exodus via the drop route. Doc Kennon made out a new seating chart which moved everyone down to the front half of the room. Hardly anyone slipped out anymore.

Doc Kennon had been at the University since the early years of the century and he sprinkled his lecture with references and stories from his early days. We might be dealing with some theory on star formation when something would trigger his memory and we would get a story that usually had nothing to do with the current lecture topic. We enjoyed them and, upon reflection, most of them presented some principle or lesson which would have lifetime application. A few of them I still remember.

In those early days, Astronomy was part of the Math Department, and Doc Kennon taught math and several other science courses in addition to Astronomy. Without a doubt, he had a broad math/science education. One day he got off on a familiar geometric theorem.

"You know, class, I taught geometry here for many years and for a long time there was one theorem that gave me a lot of concern. It was theorem number five in the old Blue Book. It said, 'A straight line is the shortest distance between two points.' Well, in proving that, you never really proved that that one line was the shortest. What you did was draw a bunch of other lines and prove that they weren't the shortest and then concluded that since they weren't the shortest, your original straight line was the shortest. For some reason that always bothered me.

"Well, one day I happened to be going through the Lyceum Building when I passed by a class being taught by Dr. Hume, who most everybody considered to be the foremost math scholar on campus. The door was open and I heard him say, 'Our first topic of the day is theorem number five.' I stopped to listen. I determined to find out how this great mathematician would handle this theorem.

"Dr. Hume said, 'Class, this theorem states that a straight line is the shortest distance between two points. Well, class, we all know that any dog knows that, so we'll just move along to theorem number six.'

"From that day forward, that theorem never bothered me again. And I think we still spend too much time fiddling around with stuff everybody knows. That's what each of you need to do with your education—get out there where every dog hasn't been and do something new that's worth doing."

Not bad advice in any age.

One day Doc Kennon was talking about the vastness of the heavens and got off on how important it was for people to stretch themselves, reach out, and broaden their horizons. He told a story about his trying to do just that in his early years.

It seems that he knew the heavens, but he had never been to the West Coast. This became an obsession with him and he longed to drive as far west as possible, to drive to a beach in California and put the wheels of his car into the sunset. After a few years, he and his wife got another couple interested in driving to the West Coast and sharing expenses. They saved up, and one summer in the 1920s, they headed west. There were numerous sights to see along the way, but they were incidental to Doc Kennon. The highlight of the trip would come when he drove his wheels into the sunset.

Well, they got to their destination late one afternoon and checked into a hotel along one of the boulevards leading to the beach. The women wanted to freshen up and rest a bit, but Doc Kennon was too excited. The sun was going down and he was determined to put the wheels of his car into the sunset that very afternoon. They got the luggage unloaded and he and the other man headed for the beach, leaving the women at the hotel.

Their boulevard led directly to the beach. Doc Kennon tried to describe his feeling when he drove out on the sand and first saw the vastness of the Pacific with the sun hanging just above the horizon. After soaking up this scene for several minutes, he drove down into the sunset as far as he dared. He did get close enough for the spray to wet the hood of the car. They then drove up and down the beach, stopping to view the sunset at several points.

After the sun disappeared, they headed back to the hotel. Just then they realized they had a problem. There were several boulevards coming to the beach, and they all looked about the same. They tried several, but none looked familiar. They could have just called the hotel, but in their haste to leave, they had not written down its name. It was quite amusing hearing Doc Kennon relate how they finally got reunited with their wives. They got the police involved, but it was almost midnight before a reunion was affected.

After telling this story on himself, Doc Kennon looked around the room over his glasses and said, "Class, it's a wonderful experience to broaden your horizons and run your wheels into the sunset but it's also a good idea to remember where home base is."

Doc Kennon's story about the transient student was my favorite. I don't know what came up in class to remind him of it. Probably nothing did. He just had some stories he was going to relate when they came to mind regardless of whether they fit into the context of anything or not.

"Class, I want to tell you about a boy who came through here a few years ago and how I came to know him. It was during the Depression. That was the '30s, for those of you who don't know. It was in the summertime and I had stopped on my way home at a little coffee shop just off the town square to have a coke. This young fellow came in for a cold drink and I could see that he was upset about something. We got to talking and I found that he had just gotten a speeding ticket. Charged with doing 40 in a 30 mph zone. He said he didn't think he was speeding but had no way to prove that he wasn't, and he was now going to have to stay in town until the next court date which was one day the next week. Now, I could have told him that it didn't make any difference how fast he'd been going. At that time everybody who came through Oxford from out of state or from a faraway county in Mississippi paid a speeding fine. It was just one of the city's revenue sources.

"As it turned out, he was from up in Ohio and was trying to find a place to go to college. He was a football player and had been trying out for those coaches who'd let him. He wanted a football scholarship or some way to pay his college expenses. He had an old car he'd fixed up. He was sleeping in it and using local creeks to clean up in. When he ran low on money he'd stay awhile someplace and earn some doing odd jobs.

"I sort of took a shine to him and took him on home with me. Since he had to stay in town anyway, I told him I knew a number of people who would be glad to hire him, so he could just use this forced layover to fatten his traveling money. He wanted to sleep in his car, but we had a spare bedroom and always enough food on the table for an extra person, so I made him come into the house.

"The folks who hired him were impressed both with him and his work. I was also getting more impressed with him as the days passed.

"He was still fuming about having to pay that speeding ticket. A couple of days before the court date I told him that I couldn't see but one way to beat the speeding charge. I said to him, 'Son, will your car go more than 30 miles an hour?' He said that he was sure that it would. I said, 'Well, we'll just have to see that it won't. You bring your car with me and let's leave it today with a fellow I know.' He did, and I told my friend what we needed. When we picked it up that afternoon, he said everything seemed to be just fine.

"The traffic judge seemed surprised when the boy pleaded 'not guilty' to the speeding charge. 'On what grounds?' he asked. 'On the grounds that my car won't go over 30 miles an hour,' he replied. The judge looked at him for a few seconds and then asked for his keys. He gave them to two deputies who were standing by and told them to take it out and see what it'd do. They came back after about thirty minutes and reported that the one time they'd gotten it above 30 was coming down that long hill on Highway 6 east of town. The judge didn't have any choice except to dismiss the charges. He gave me a pretty hard look when he banged his gavel, but I figured justice had been done.

"With the ticket behind us, I talked to some of the football coaches and other folks in the Athletic Department.

They arranged a tryout and agreed to give him some scholarship help. I also talked to some other people around campus and they managed to come up with enough jobs for him to pay the rest of his expenses.

"Now, I wish I could tell you that this young man became an outstanding ball player and led our team to all sorts of victories. He didn't. But I can tell you that for four straight years he was the best and hardest working player on our scout team. And I think there's something to be said for that.

"He may not have been a great ball player, but he was a great student and he made a number of positive contributions to the University while he was here. Graduated with a degree in engineering. Served with an engineer outfit in Europe during World War II. Has a good job with a big firm out West. I still hear from him after all these years."

After relating this story, Doc Kennon folded his arms, leaned back against his lecture table, and surveyed the room over his glasses for several seconds before observing, "Class, this is a great country and you can still be successful here *if* you've got enough backbone."

When I sat in his class, Doc Kennon was very close to the end of a very long and illustrious teaching career. I sometimes shudder to think just how close I came to missing him altogether. I would have had it not been for the juxtaposition of several things at the same time. However, the ones I really feel sorry for are those who sat in the class and still missed him.

19
The Preparation

Back in the '50s I bowled on a team which was sponsored by a local dry cleaners. Tom was one of the team members and was a good bowler. Carried about a 190 average. Tom was young and had been married less than a year when his wife became pregnant. They wanted children and were happy about becoming parents, but Tom couldn't figure out how he was going to pay the hospital and doctor bills, since he wasn't making much money and had no medical insurance.

He gave this matter a great deal of serious thought and came up with a plan. He knew that the bills were unavoidable, so he set about finding out ways to cut these costs. Figuring that there were some things which could be eliminated, or at least have their cost reduced, he went first to his wife's doctor and explained what he wanted to do. The doctor made up a list of his normal charges and worked with Tom on a cost reduction plan.

Tom's next stop was the county hospital. The hospital administrator was equally cooperative. He had the business office prepare an itemized list of charges for a normal delivery and then sat down with Tom to go over the list, line by line. This list was much longer than the doctor's and Tom was effecting some savings when they came to the line that read, "Preparation. . . $10.00."

"What's that?" asked Tom. The administrator explained that that was the shaving off of the pubic hair just before delivery. "Any reason why I can't do that?" was Tom's next question. The administrator said that he knew of no reason why he couldn't, so Tom put "preparation" on his list of things to do.

As the bowling season and the pregnancy both advanced, we all got weekly updates on his wife's progress. We went through morning sickness, swelling feet, too much weight gain, unnatural cravings, and many other aspects. This was Tom's first exposure to the many facets of a pregnancy and he was fascinated by all of them. Finally, the doctor told him it was time for "the Preparation."

That evening after supper, Tom made ready. He got several plastic cleaner bags he'd been saving and covered a portion of the bed. These were covered with bath towels. He placed a couple of pillows where her head would be to make his wife more comfortable and then got her in position. He brought a basin of warm water, wash cloths, scissors, a safety razor, and shaving cream, and set about his task.

Things went fairly rapidly at first but slowed considerably as operations became more delicate.

In order to understand what happened next, you have to have seen a man contort his mouth to one side or the other to pull the skin tight and to smooth out the creases as he shaves around it with a safety razor.

Tom's progress was getting slower and slower. Finally, he raised up so that he could see his wife's face over her ample abdomen. "Honey," he said.

“Yes.” Using his facial muscles, Tom stretched his mouth to one side of his face. "Can you make it do this one time?"

20
Low Gas Level

I didn't know what to expect. Although I knew the father, I'd never had a conference with him. He'd left the education of his children up to his wife. I had no way of knowing if he considered this to be "woman's work," or if they had just decided to divide up family responsibilities this way. But, whenever the boy had problems, it was always the mother who came for the conference. She was a career woman in her own right and generally had to make special arrangements, but she always came. Now she couldn't come anymore. Cancer had taken her almost a year ago, and if anybody came now, it had to be the father.

The boy wasn't really a bad kid. He was the type I generally classified as "trifling" in that he wasn't too particular about obeying rules or of doing much academic work. This was a chronic condition with him. We'd been working hard on the behavior part and had been able to effect some improvement there, but the academic part was in a real mess. His mother had been a stabilizing force for him and even with all her efforts, she'd only been able to keep him at a borderline level academically. With her death, he'd fallen far below that line and no one could see any prospects of a reversal. Hence, the parent conference in the Principal's office with all his teachers.

As I said, I did not know what to expect. The father had not sounded too cordial over the phone when he found out he was going to have to put the conference in his schedule. But, he had done it. I wondered what his demeanor would be. I wondered if he might want to place the blame on the boy's teachers, or me, or himself for not being around much, or the unfairness of the world for taking his wife in her prime, or the boy himself. It would be interesting to see which direction our conference would take.

I had the chairs arranged in an oval. I sat at one end and placed the father in the first chair to my left, the boy in the first chair to my right. There were two or three chairs for the teachers. I explained the procedure. The father appeared to be in a pretty good mood. The boy was apprehensive, as well he should have been.

The first teacher came in, noted the low grade, and pointed out the reasons for it. She used such phrases as "fails to do homework" and "refuses to read assigned material." The father asked her a question or two as his face began to show an expression of concern.

Two others teachers entered just as the first was finishing. They said much the same things and added "refuses to complete work," "will not pay attention in class," and "often sleeps in class."

The father looked at the boy and asked, "Son, is what they're saying true?"

"Yes sir."

I noted that a vein was beginning to stand out on the father's neck and that he was clenching and unclenching his fists.

The last two teachers didn't do anything to ease the father's tension. They reiterated most of what had already been said and added "disrupts class," "totally disinterested in studying seriously," "never comes for help."

By this time the father was about to explode. Veins were standing out all over his neck and head. He was a weightlifter and bodybuilder and had massive arms and shoulders. I could see the definition of his arm muscles as they swelled and strained against his shirt. The buttons on the front were having a hard time restraining his chest. I was beginning to have some concern about what he might do.

The boy showed the same concern, but to a much greater degree. His father's clenched teeth and glare made him wish to be most anyplace else. He was sitting up straight in his chair with his back pressed hard against the chair back and his feet flat on the floor. Every movement by his father caused him to press harder against the back of the chair as he tried to increase the distance between them. He couldn't, but he kept trying. His eyes were wide and staring straight ahead, seeing everything and nothing at the same time.

The father was getting so worked up that I was fearful of what he might do to the boy. And if he did decide to do something violent, I couldn't figure out how I was going to stop him.

When the door closed behind the last departing teacher, the father moved suddenly and closed the gap between himself and the boy. He didn't stand up. He didn't move the chair. He just came straight across and ended up in a half squat with his hands on his thighs just above his knees and his face so close to the boy's that their noses were almost in contact. I'm sure I jumped, but he wasn't paying any attention to me.

"Son, you know what's wrong with you?!" His words

were not spoken, but were spat out through clenched teeth.

“N-n-no sir.”

"Your give-a-shit level is low!!"

The father's succinct and accurate assessment of the problem broke the tension. I had a hard time keeping from laughing out loud.

“Y-y-yes sir.”

This done, the father backed himself into his chair without removing his withering stare from his son. The boy was still pressing so hard on the chair back that you could almost see the outline of it coming through on his chest. I made a summation and ended the conference as gracefully as I could.

I wish I would report that the conference was the turning point in this young man's life. But it wasn't. He ended up flunking out of school and having to get a GED diploma. He tried college and flunked out as well. But, then, something must have awakened him because he went to another college and not only stayed in, but also did rather well. The last time I heard about him he was in medical school. Quite a distance from that day in my office.

But, still, the most memorable thing about that boy was the acronym coined by his father. From that day forward, when we encountered a student with a similar approach to his studies, we would say, "He's having a problem with a low gas level."

21
Dr. Green

I had done reasonably well in Freshman composition. Supposedly, it was the most feared course at Ole Miss, but I had bested it easily. Of course, I had gone into the course with a good working knowledge of grammar and, somewhere along the line, I had learned how to put words together pretty well. Even the second semester, which involved a research paper, was not a major challenge. I had never written a term paper in high school, but our instructor gave us a detailed outline and a schedule to follow. Anybody who could write and follow directions could do well. He even allowed me to write on the history of baseball, a sport I dearly loved. It was hard to understand where all the horror stories had come from.

However, the sophomore year worried me. Coming up was a year of English literature, or "Soph. Lit." as it was generally called. And I had good reason to be fearful of it.

I'm sure my high school teachers had done the best they could with what they had to work with. But, one of the main things I discovered during my freshman year was what they hadn't taught me. I knew I knew grammar and could write a little, but we had done little or no literary analysis or criticism, and had read none of the major works in their entirety. Our reading was limited to the brief excerpts in the lit books. At that point in my life, literature was a vast, uncharted sea and I feared my boat wasn't very seaworthy.

So, I set about doing the best I could with the only element over which I had any control: which professor to sign up for. In my research among the older students, one name kept cropping up--Dr. Green. Nobody said he was easy. They just said you could pass his class. However, there was one disadvantage--he only taught one section and it met on that dreaded TTS schedule (Tuesday, Thursday, Saturday). This was back in the dark ages when colleges scheduled regular classes on Saturday. It seemed as if each department had its quota of TTS classes to fill. It was rumored that the English Department kept Dr. Green's sophomore lit class there because it always filled, helping to meet the quota. I vowed not to let that stand in my way.

In those days all registration was done by hand over a two-day period in alphabetical order starting with "A" one semester and "Z" the next. The more popular classes were usually filled early the first day. With a "B" name and a "Z" schedule, I was trying to figure some way to get into the line early when fate smiled down on me. Since Coach Vaught was concerned about having his two-a-day practices interrupted over a two-day period with registration, he prevailed upon the Registrar to allow the football team and all those associated with it to register early.

They turned us into the gym about an hour before anyone else. I grabbed up the necessary papers at the door and made a beeline for the English table. A line was already forming, but when I got to the table, Dr. Green's TTS lit class was still open. I had my class.

At first glance, Dr. Green was rather ordinary looking. He was about six feet tall, and I guessed him to be about fifty or so. His head was topped by a shock of mostly gray hair which usually needed the attention of a comb. A closely cropped mustache was the same color as his hair. The most distinguishing characteristic about him was the shape of his head. It gave the appearance of having developed within the confines of a large vise. It was the most elongated head I'd ever seen. The distance from front to rear was probably twice the distance from temple to temple. I wondered how he ever found a hat to fit him.

He spoke "in drama." Not unlike an actor on stage. Every sentence was filled with adjectives and adverbs and their use was accompanied by appropriate hand gestures, head movements, and facial expressions. For reasons I had not yet come to understand, prose and poetry excited him and he was determined to transmit his excitement to a group of mostly disinterested college sophomores.

He did all of this in a voice that was most unusual. It was like no other voice I'd ever heard and I've never heard one since that came close to matching it. There was a touch of British in it, but only a touch. It was a voice that, once heard, was never forgotten.

Dr. Green had been on Eisenhower's staff in England during World War II. In what capacity, I never learned. He was a bird colonel in the reserves and occasionally taught a course in the ROTC Department. On these teaching days, he came to class in his dress uniform with all the campaign ribbons, wearing the eagles on his shoulders. Somehow I was never able to reconcile the military man with the one who roved about the classroom waving his arms in excitement over some poem or work of literature.

The tone for the class was set early in the semester. Boykin was married and lived on campus in married student housing. He had a large black bloodhound that often followed him to school and, as a result, had become quite well-known on campus. On this particular day, the dog had followed him into Dr. Green's class and was stretched out in the back sound asleep. Dr. Green was calling the roll and trying to place a face with each name in his grade book when he spotted the dog. He recoiled as if he'd seen a black panther readying itself to pounce. He leaned backwards, his hands extended forward to ward off the attack, and with raised eyebrows and wide eyes, exclaimed in his best dramatic voice, "Gad!! What is this I spy? Can it be a mastiff about to attack? "

All eyes turned to the rear as an embarrassed Boykin jumped out of his seat, grabbed the dog's collar, and started leading him out of the room. "He's mine, Dr. Green. I'll get him out and I promise you I won't let him come back." Boykin needed to pass this course and he surely did not want to incur the wrath of its teacher. But Dr. Green's next words stopped him in his tracks.

"No! No! No! He's such a splendid animal. A magnificent beast. I've seen him around. It's an honor to have him come to class. Let him stay. What's his name?"

"Jack, sir," replied Boykin still looking rather apprehensive.

"Jack! Wonderful name. Bring him often. I'll put him on the roll." With that, Dr. Green took his pen and added Jack to the end of his roster.

Boykin led Jack back to his place where he flopped down and was back to sleep in a matter of seconds.

Except for those Saturdays when we were out of town on a football trip, Boykin made sure he brought Jack to class every day. And at the end of roll call, Dr. Green always called, "Jack."

"He's here, Dr. Green."

"Splendid," would be the reply as Jack's presence was recorded.

At the end of the course, I think Jack had a better attendance record than some of the students. Boykin often said that Jack got him through English Lit, but I think it was because Boykin went to class most every day since he had to take Jack. I've often wondered if Dr. Green didn't know Boykin's record and just used Jack to get him to class so he could teach him something. At any rate, we learned early in the course that Dr. Green had another side which differed markedly from the "learned professor" and the "bird colonel" image.

Poetry

Dr. Green loved poetry. He loved to teach poetry. But, most of all, he loved to read poetry out loud and with expression. He loved to teach the meter of poetry. As I recall, he was especially partial to iambic pentameter, with which he satisfied both his love for teaching and reading.

"Can't you just feel the rhythm?" he would exude as he clasped the book to his breast, his eyes cast upward toward the irregularly shaped water marks on the ceiling. For those of us who couldn't, he would exclaim, "Just listen to the beat!" He would follow this with a reading of a portion of the work, giving exaggerated emphasis to the accented syllables. For added emphasis, he would stand beside his desk and kick it in the side with his off foot on these syllables. The desk was just a light classroom desk, and Dr. Green put a lot of vigor into his strokes; so much, in fact, that the desk would move several inches with each blow. When he ran out of room going one direction on a longer work, Dr. Green would move to the opposite side of the desk and, without missing a word, begin kicking it back in the opposite direction with his other foot. He got equal distance with either foot and on a good day, the desk might make four or five trips across the front of the room.

I never ceased to marvel how he could kick, shuffle along sideways to keep up with the desk, never miss a word, and still read with intensity and feeling. You could never say Dr. Green's class was dull.

One day Dr. Green brought a small volume of poetry to class and was reading a poem from it to illustrate some poetic point he was trying to make. As usual, he read with feeling. I've long since forgotten the poem, poet, and point he was illustrating. However, the ending was unforgettable. As he neared the end, his voice began to rise in both intensity and in volume. The last line was something like, "and the devil take it," which was delivered at a shout. As he began that line, Dr. Green suddenly drew back and threw the book at the rear wall. There was a girl sitting in the seat in the right rear corner who had dozed off. The volume of the last line had startled her awake and, as she jerked her head up, all she saw was Dr. Green in his follow-through and the book sailing over her head with its pages fluttering like a wounded quail. The book made a perfect two-rail bank off the corner of the room and hit her in back of the head. She jumped to her feet and screamed.

"Splendid reaction!" exclaimed Dr. Green, who apparently did not realize she had been asleep.

As he retrieved his book and placed its pages back into order, he explained that when the author had given the first public reading of the poem, she had thrown the manuscript into the audience in just that fashion.

No, Dr. Green's class was never dull.

A Survey of British Literature

The official title of the course was "A Survey of British Literature," and survey we did. We began with the very early pieces like *Beowulf*. I especially liked the monster, Grendel. Before long we arrived at Chaucer's century and paused for a time with *The Canterbury Tales*. We were never allowed to read such bawdy stories in high school. I even read some of the tales that were not assigned, probably my first major foray into extra academic work.

Dr. Green loved the Middle English in which Chaucer wrote. He would often quote or read a passage from the tale we were discussing in that language, and after finishing would say something like "Exquisite, beautiful, don't you agree?" We usually did, even though we'd hardly understood a word he'd uttered.

Because he was such a lover of Chaucer's language, Dr. Green tried to pass along some of his love to his students. "*Of course*, you all will want to memorize the first eighteen lines of 'The Prologue' in the original. You will love it." We knew this was not an option but a required assignment, and our loving it was doubtful at this stage.

Whan that Aprill with his shoures soote

The droghte of March hath perced to the roote,

And bathed every veyne in swich licour

Of which vertu engendred is the flour;

But, memorize we did, and even with all the reluctance, we had to admit the language did have a wonderful sound. However, many questioned why in the world we had to memorize a passage which would obviously be of absolutely no use in the future. Dr. Green seemed to sense this feeling, so one day he told us a story. And, I might add, that he told his stories with the same feeling and drama with which he read poetry.

"Now, students, I know some of you think the memorizing of these first eighteen lines is foolish and you are not doing it with much enthusiasm. Well, let me tell you what happened to me one night in London during the War.

"I was on my way to dinner when air-raid sirens sounded. The city went immediately to total blackout conditions. The German bombers could be heard in the distance. I changed directions and headed for the nearest shelter. As I hurried along in total darkness, I ran headlong into another chap going in the opposite direction. Our collision knocked him to the pavement. I said, 'Oh, pardon me. I'm so sorry,' to which he replied as he struggled to his feet, 'My God! I don't believe it! It can't be!' I had no idea what he meant. I sensed that he was searching in his pockets for a light of some kind. Of course, a light of any kind was contrary to regulations and I was about to tell him so when I heard a Zippo lighter being opened. He held it up near my face, lit it, and exclaimed, 'But it is!' Then he began to recite:

Whan that Aprill with his shoures soote

The droghte of March hath perced to the roote,

"It was one my former students who had not forgotten his Chaucer. He doused the light and we went arm-in-arm to the shelter. Had a wonderful visit there during the air raid. Afterward he joined me for dinner. We had roast duck as I remember. A delightful evening.

"So, you see students, I can truthfully say to you, you just never know when a familiarity with Chaucer might come in handy."

Yes, Dr. Green was an unusual teacher. I did well in his class, but besides that, he passed on some of his love for language, love for literature, and love for life and living. I still remember his face and I know that after forty-five years, I'd still recognize his distinctive voice. And I'm proud of the fact that I can still quote some of the lines from "The Prologue" in Chaucer's language.

22
The Wedding

Truman did not like weddings. In fact, he despised them. In his view the only weddings a man should be required to attend would be his own and those of his natural children. But in his life things hadn't worked out that way. After his and Marnell's there were weddings of their friends to which Marnell said, "We just have to go." After this flurry of activity, there was a lull. But then came the children of these friends. Now that this second generation of nuptials had about run its course, Truman resented Marnell's dragging him to what he termed "extraneous ceremonies" of folks they hardly knew.

The main thing Truman had against weddings was when they occurred. "Is there some law," he once asked Marnell, "that requires all weddings to be held on Saturday?" They tended to conflict with his Saturday mornings of golf followed by afternoons of watching football and other sports at the Club with his friends.

The reception food was another problem. Truman disliked trying to find something edible among the mostly unidentifiable offerings. It seemed to him that caterers tried to outdo each other in putting non-compatible items together. Marnell always said, "Just make another trip through the line and we won't have to have supper." But Truman did not count mystery finger food and pastel colored punch consumed standing up as a real meal. Their differing views had produced many strained weekends over the years.

Of course, Marnell loved weddings as much as Truman hated them. She always cried. One of her maxims was, "All brides are beautiful." One Saturday when she made this observation about a particularly homely bride, Truman could restrain himself no longer.

"Aw, come on, Marnell, your eyes aren't that bad. That girl's a mud fence. That's like you always saying the same thing about babies. Last week when you told old Callaway how pretty his new grandson was I nearly choked. That kid looks like a Sun Sweet prune with hair." Marnell's only response was to scoot away from him on the pew and dab at her eyes with a tissue. Truman braced himself for another testy weekend.

But the straw that broke the proverbial camel's back was Satterfield, a middle-aged man who worked in Marnell's office. His wife died and members of his church took turns bringing him meals, cleaning his house, and doing other things to help him in his bereavement. At least they took turns until Almeda came upon the scene. Her husband had run off with a barmaid several years earlier and she was looking for some security. Marnell brought home a step-by-step account of Almeda's pursuit and capture of Satterfield. Truman followed the process with sardonic glee little realizing that he would be a witness to the final ceremony.

Almeda began to come to Satterfield's home more and more frequently to clean and cook and always to comfort. After a few weeks, she began to stay over at night "just for convenience." It was not long until two or three nights in a row became more "convenient."

"It's like watching a bull being led to slaughter,"

observed Truman.

The "courtship" became a daily topic of conversation. Truman couldn't see what Almeda saw in Satterfield. "He's not much to look at and he's already had to declare bankruptcy once. If that's security for her, she must be as poor as Job's turkey," noted Truman one evening.

"Well, he does make a good salary. Maybe she will be able to help him manage it better. And, anyway, she does own some property," Marnell responded as she came to Almeda's defense.

"Property? Where?" asked Truman.

"An uncle left her forty acres over near Cedartown."

"Does she own a mule, too?" asked Truman sarcastically as he alluded to the hollow promise of "forty acres and a mule" to the freed slaves at the end of the Civil War.

"No. The ground's too rocky and poor in that area. But she does have a goat."

"A goat!" howled Truman as he doubled over with laughter. "Why I'm sure she'll soon be a major shipper to the Chicago stockyards." Marnell tossed her head and stalked out of the room. From then on, Truman always referred to Almeda's forty acres as "The Ponderosa" and when he really wanted to tease Marnell about the situation, he'd ask, "Say, how's that goat doing?"

But the day of reckoning came one evening as Marnell casually announced "Satterfield and Almeda are getting married the sixteenth of next month and we've been invited and we need to go."

Truman roared like a bear caught in a trap. "What do you mean, 'we need to go'?" They're not my friends. I don't work with either of them"

"Well now," Marnell replied calmly, "You know none of the men in the office care for Satterfield, so they're not going. Somebody from the office needs to go and show him some support."

"How did you get elected?" asked Truman rhetorically. "I'll bet that's a Saturday." Truman went to his desk and scanned his calendar. "It sure is. What about my golf? And UT has a late afternoon kick off and I'll probably miss all of the game. Why don't you just go by yourself?"

"I can't. It's at Cedartown."

"Cedartown!" Truman was floundering about like a large mouth bass with a plug in his mouth he couldn't shake. "That's at least an hour and a half away. It's so far back in the sticks I don't think the State has even built roads there yet. And I know they don't have churches. Isn't that one of the places our church sent a mission team to last summer to bring the gospel to the natives?"

"Aw, quit exaggerating. You've made so much fun of this whole thing until you deserve to see just how nice everything turns out. Just put the wedding on your calendar. It's at 4:00 o'clock."

All Truman could do was whimper. He knew he was beaten.

On the sixteenth Marnell caught him trying to sneak his small radio with the earplug into the car. "It'll just fit in my inside pocket and with the earplug nobody'll be able to hear it but me and this is an important game." Marnell made sure it stayed home.

Even Truman had to admit that it was a pretty drive to Cedartown. They made good time, arrived early, and pulled into a parking spot beside the church to wait. There were only three or four other cars.

As they sat in the car, the side door to the church opened and a boy of about sixteen or seventeen walked out on the landing of the side steps. He had on a plaid, short-sleeve sport shirt, jeans, and brown loafers with white socks. "That's Satterfield's son," noted Marnell. "He's going to be the best man."

"I'm glad he got dressed early for the ceremony." Truman thought he was being facetious.

When the boy turned around, a telltale circle could be seen on the left rear pocket of his jeans. He slipped a can of Skoal out of this repository, opened it, and put a dip in his cheek. "Wonder where he'll spit during the ceremony?" mused Truman.

"You're just impossible," scolded Marnell, "let's go inside."

The church was old and the auditorium sort of rambled off in several directions. It was obvious that there would not be many in attendance. Every sound seemed to echo around the irregular room.

There was a rather large, clumsy man klunking around in the choir area. He was setting up a TV camera in the back corner and was having some difficulty getting it focused. This called for numerous trips back and forth. The loudness of his footfalls on the uncarpeted choir tiers was only exceeded by his kicking of two or three chairs on each trip. Truman expected to see him trip and fall in amongst the chairs at every passage but he somehow managed to keep his balance.

Other guests began to arrive. Several had children of various ages. One lady came in with a child who looked to be about a year old in one arm and some type of round, folded up contraption in the other. "What's that thing?" asked Marnell. "That's one of those round walkers on wheels," replied Truman. "She's going to turn that kid loose on everyone during the reception." Marnell looked aghast. "Surely not," she said.

A woman got up to sing. She was a little off key and she and the organist had not practiced together enough. At times the singer was ahead; at others, the organist was in the lead. Occasionally their musical paths crossed but they never remained together for long. During the songs, the TV man continued his focusing trips. The children talked, kicked the pews, and cried. The service was beginning to sound like an Arabian market place.

"Why did she want to do this?" Truman whispered.

Marnell whispered back, "She didn't have a real wedding the first time so she's determined to have one this go around."

"Some people just don't know when they're well off," thought Truman to himself.

The singer got through singing. Shortly thereafter the organist got through playing. The minister, Satterfield, and his son entered through a side door and came down front.

Truman's mouth fell open. The boy wore the same clothes except he had added a loud, stripped tie to go with the plaid shirt. The can of Skoal still protruded from his rear pocket. As far as Truman could tell, he did not have a dip in his cheek.

The organist began to play the preliminary "bride's gonna be coming soon" music. "Who's gonna give her away?" Truman whispered. "Nobody," answered Marnell. "She's having her grandchildren bring her down the aisle."

"Well, at least it'll be something different," responded Truman.

When the organist hit the first notes of "Here Comes the Bride," the scene suddenly went from the ridiculous to the absurd. The guests turned to the rear. The back door burst open and Almeda's four grandchildren exploded into the sanctuary like a covey of quail coming out of a patch of broom sedge. Almeda, framed in the doorway, paused for effect and for pictures while the four (ages two to four) began to run back and forth across the rear of the church squealing at the top of their lungs. The only thing visible to the guests was the tops of the children's heads as they sped to and fro. This unforeseen turn forced Almeda to abandon her picture pose and try to round up the errant kids. She began grabbing them one at a time as they raced past her and within a couple of minutes had them all corralled. After getting them settled down, she swept down the aisle, holding on to two of them with each hand.

Truman was laughing so hard that he was shaking the pew. Marnell kept jabbing him in the ribs but there was so much other commotion going on that no one really was paying any attention to him.

Almeda finally got her troops in place in front of the minister. Somehow those standing down front had managed to maintain their composure. "Dearly beloved," the minister began. Klunk, klunk, klunk—The TV man was checking his camera again. The minister paused, turned, and glared at him, but the TV man intent on his equipment continued his mission without noticing.

Giving up, the minister continued but most of the guests' attention was focused on the grandchildren who were playing hide-and-seek with Almeda's billowing skirt. Two of the smaller ones even got under it and ran around. It looked like two cats fighting in a sack. Truman hoped that the TV camera was recording all this.

At this point Marnell tuned away from Truman, buried her face in her hands, and began to shake. Truman had seen her cry at weddings but he had never seen her body so racked by sobs. As he patted her on the back to console her, he realized that she was not crying but laughing uncontrollably. He wanted to say, "I told you so," but thought better of it and just continued to pat.

Mercifully, the ceremony came to an end and Marnell got herself under control. Truman did not let on that he knew she was not crying. Before anyone could get out of the sanctuary, the TV man began kicking over chairs as he took down his equipment.

Truman and Marnell headed downstairs to the fellowship hall for the reception. As they started through the door, Truman heard a sound not unlike a subway train coming out of a tunnel. He jerked Marnell back just in time to keep her from being run down by the kid in the rolling walker. He might not have been able to walk but he could propel that walker around the hall's tile floor like a low-level missile. He spent most of the reception ricocheting off table legs and the shins of non-wary guests.

The reception refreshments showed Almeda's influence. There was red punch, salted nuts, cake, and <u>ice cream</u>. According to Almeda, "You must have ice cream with cake." It was a disaster. The serving ladies had gotten the ice cream out too soon and it was almost melted when they served it. This caused it to run off the little flat glass plates. The adults had problems keeping it on their plates; most of the children could not even if they tried. The result was a floor with a lot of melted ice cream on it plus some cake fragments. The only good thing was that the sticky floor slowed down the kid in the rolling walker.

As Marnell had predicted, no one else from the office came. Satterfield seemed appreciative of their effort and thanked them two or three times for attending. Truman felt a little better knowing he had contributed to making Satterfield feel better.

As they drove away from the church, Truman resisted the temptation to tease Marnell about her breakdown of laughter.

"I wonder where they'll spend their honeymoon," mused Marnell.

"Probably at The Ponderosa," replied Truman.

"No, I don't think so."

"Why not?"

Marnell looked at Truman and a half smile came to her lips. "The goat died last week."

23
The Hokey-Pokey

Spring 1997. The junior-senior prom. For those educators at the secondary level, this annual rite of spring is all too familiar. Black seemed to be the color of choice this year for a majority of the young ladies. Some of the young men came up with new steps and a few even had whole routines which no one had seen before. But after living through the Twist, The Swim, The Watusi and a whole host of other dances whose names I cannot remember and whose moves are indescribable, nothing is very unusual or shocking. However, I do admit that I really do have a problem understanding slam-dancing.

Late, that evening I did get one surprise. In fact, it was such a big surprise that it could be classified as a shock. I heard a familiar tune and saw familiar moves on the dance floor. I felt as if I were in a time warp. They may have been doing it as a novelty, but there, right before my eyes, were these present-day teenagers doing a dance that we had done in the late 1940s at a small high school in Mississippi. I wondered if these kids knew that they were doing a dance that their grandparents had done fifty years ago. But there was no mistaking it. They were doing the Hokey-Pokey and appeared to be enjoying it.

For those of you unfamiliar with this exotic dance, let me explain. The Hokey-Pokey is best performed in a circle. The participants not only dance, but sing the lyrics for the dance, which is a roll-call for various body parts. We always began ours with "right arm" and the lyrics went:

You put your right arm in.

You take your right arm out.

You put your right arm in

and you shake it all about.

Then, you do the hokey-pokey,

And you turn yourself around,

That's what it's all about.

Then you would repeat with the next body part. Our sequence after "right arm" was "left arm, right elbow, left elbow, right leg, left leg, right hip, left hip, head, backside, and whole self."

It was a rather repetitious dance, but a person could be very creative on the "shake it all about," "do the hokey-pokey," and "turn yourself around" parts. In fact, I think we raised this dance to an art form in my high school. We didn't just do the dance—we specialized.

There were no formal contests or rules at the beginning. Kids just began to develop special moves with certain body parts and before long there was general recognition that Bobby did the best left arm, Sally had the best right leg, etc. The girls seemed to have the best hip moves, a fact that was both recognized and admired by most of the young men.

The craze spread rapidly through my small high school and soon we recognized a boy and a girl champion for each body part. As the interest grew, challenges began to be issued to the champions. This resulted in a set of rules for champions and challengers alike. Although not in written form, they were known by all and enforced by the entire dancing community.

Most dances were challenge dances, with the Hokey-Pokey being performed three or four times during the evening. If you were a champion, you had to be present to defend. An absent champion's body part was up for grabs and went to the best performer at that particular dance. A challenge was issued by stepping into the circle next to the champion and announcing such. The winner was determined by applause from those present. A dethroned champion could not ask for a rematch that same evening. He had to wait at least until the next dance. The last Hokey-Pokey of the evening was a dance for champions. Only they performed, there would be no challenges, and it was generally a sight to behold.

The Homecoming Dance, the Christmas Dance, and the Junior-Senior Prom were all non-challenge dances. Everybody wanted to be reigning champion going into those dances. If you were, you could really show off in front of a large crowd without the worry of being dethroned.

After many hours of private practice, I mounted a successful challenge and became boys' backside champion early in my senior year. During the year, I successfully fought off all challenges due mainly to the facility I developed of shaking each cheek independently of the other. No other boy was able to overcome this rather distinct advantage. A few years later I noted that this talent was possessed by any number of female exotic dancers, although I doubted that they had learned this while doing the Hokey-Pokey.

My senior year really went well. I had good grades in all my courses and I successfully defended my backside championship at every dance. However, little did I realize that a catastrophe was lurking just over the horizon, poised to strike at the worst possible moment.

It happened at the last dance before the Junior-Senior prom. This was the last Hokey-Pokey challenge dance of the year and every champion knew there would be numerous challenges. And to the winners went the spoils. The champions at this point could really say that they were the best of that school year. They got to perform without challenges at the biggest dance of the year. Since senior champions would not be back the next year, they got the honor of retiring as champions.

There were a few successful challenges for other body parts, but no one came close to knocking me off my throne. By this time I was getting a little cocky, and not only attempted, but also made some moves that even I did not think I was capable of.

Then the last Hokey-Pokey of the evening was announced—the dance for champions only. When the music started, we all hit the circle with a great sense of pride. We would be the main attraction at the prom in five weeks and, at this point, *nobody* could take that away from us. At least we *thought* nobody could.

The dance was a spirited one, as these champion dances usually were. Every body part garnered a significant amount of applause. My body part was close to the end, and energy seemed to be building inside of me as we neared this point. On the second "put your backside in" line, all this pent-up energy seemed to explode. Although I was not familiar with the term at that time, I may have experienced an adrenaline rush of epic proportions. Anyway, I jumped high into the air, turned 180 degrees, and landed in the center of the circle. Unbeknownst to me and without any prearrangement, Ora Jean Caldwell, the girls' backside champion, who was directly across the circle from me, did the same thing. There we were, back-to-back. Neither of us knew the other was there until we bent over and our backsides seemed to fuse. And when we "shook it all about," I felt tingling sensations running down my legs and up my back. I thought I was in love for the first time, but when we began a new unit in physics the next week, I discovered that it was only static electricity. The lights were dim and some who were in the right position swore they saw sparks. I can't speak for Ora Jean, but for me it was a transcendent experience.

Before the dance was over, the two main chaperons, Miss Adams and Miss Jefferson, were on Ora Jean and me like two ducks after June bugs. We called them the founding mothers. They were both old maids of considerable years. They seemed to live for two things: teaching English and guiding the moral development of all teenagers. They were at every dance to ensure the latter. Neither approved of slow dances, when couples tended to get too close together, and they had banished dipping some years earlier. The Hokey-Pokey was on their approved list because there was almost no contact between the two sexes. At least there was not until Ora Jean and I got ourselves into such an outrageous position.

We were both chided severely that evening and we thought that would be the end of it. But it was not so. On

Monday the founding mothers took us to the Principal's office and proceeded to get us banned from the Junior-Senior prom. If that wasn't bad enough, they also succeeded in getting the Hokey-Pokey banned as well. It was now an outlaw dance that could not be performed at any school function.

The Hokey-Pokey ban affected a lot of people. And they all seemed to get angry with me and Ora Jean. Our class practically ostracized us for the remainder of the year. The prom was a flop without the Hokey-Pokey and its champions. Ora Jean and I were miserable for the rest of the year. We both thought that all this was a big price to have to pay for a little static electricity.

Yes, watching our kids do the Hokey-Pokey brought back a lot of memories, some good and some bad. The best of them all was of Ora Jean Caldwell and that transcendent moment when sparks flew and time stood still.

24
The Grade Book

- Reunion weekend.
- A small southern prep school.
- Yellow jonquils in full bloom.
- The plum and other flowering trees painting the campus with splashes of white and pink.
- The grass--new, green, and freshly mowed.
- Five-year reunions for classes from years ending in 7 and 2--'87, '82, '77 and on back to those early years of the century.
- A mixture of alums.
- Many at their first gathering, fresh-faced, new college graduates, easily mistaken for high school seniors.
- The number of alums getting smaller as the years' numbers grew smaller.
- Gray or bald, unsteady steps, canes, one wheelchair.

A small group in their mid to late thirties had gathered around one of their former teachers, telling stories, laughing, poking fun at each other much as they had done fifteen years earlier.

Suddenly, they realized that a new person had joined the circle. No one had seen him arrive. He just sort of appeared. He was small, nondescript, and hardly noticeable, just as he had been in high school. No one had paid him much attention then, and the years had not changed things.

The teacher remembered him. He'd been in two of his classes, always sitting off to the side; an average student, quiet, unobtrusive, hardly noticed by either teacher or students. He had been sent to boarding school by his mother who lived several states away. She was divorced for about the third time and had neither the time nor inclination to raise a teenage son. So the boy divided his time between boarding school and summer camps.

The laughing and joking ceased abruptly, all eyes focused on the new arrival. He didn't seem to notice the attention or, if he did, he gave no indication. He spoke to none of the group even though some had been classmates. He fixed the teacher with a gaze that was both piercing and pleading. "I hoped you'd be here," he said.

"I'm glad you came back," the teacher replied. "Glad" was too strong a word, but he could not think of one that would fit.

"I brought something back," he said as he took a large, brown envelope from under his arm and handed it to the teacher.

With a look of puzzlement on his face, the teacher pulled up the little metal retainers, opened the flap, and pulled out a grade book. It took a few seconds for the teacher to realize just what he was holding. It was not just any grade book; it was the missing grade book.

The teacher was one who kept things. His career spanned almost thirty years and several schools. One thing that he kept was his grade books. They were lined up in order on a high shelf in his little cubbyhole office next to his classroom. For anyone wanting to know what Osgood Willingham had done in Algebra II on 14 March 1963, the record was there. The teacher took a certain pride in this. Occasionally, he would take one down, flip through it, and reflect on those students and that particular year. But one was missing.

The teacher prided himself on not losing things. He kept things in order and he expected the same of his students. This made the year his grade book disappeared stand out vividly. It was shortly after the end of school. The students had gone and everything was finished. As he tidied up his room and put things in his office for the summer, there was no grade book. He always kept it either in or on his desk. He even checked to see if he'd added it to his collection on the shelf out of habit and forgotten, but such was not the case. He searched his classroom, his office and his home, asked other teachers, and poked through the trash, but to no avail. Over the years he could never resign himself to the fact that there were only twenty-seven grade books for his twenty-eight years. And now, after fifteen years, here was the missing grade book.

As the teacher stood holding the green-covered book, it dawned on him what must have happened. "You stole my grade book?" The teacher's words carried no hint of anger or accusation, only a groping for an explanation.

As this two-person drama unfolded, the others, with uncomfortable glances at each other, drifted away leaving the two by themselves.

"It was after the graduation ceremonies. Several of my classmates were in your classroom saying good-bye and talking about college and their plans for the summer. I don't think anyone noticed when I came in. I didn't plan on taking it or anything else, but as I stood there outside the group, I had an overwhelming desire to leave with something important. Your grade book was there on the corner of your desk. We all knew how important it was to you. The next thing I knew I was outside with it under my arm."

As the young man spoke, the two had begun to walk slowly across the campus.

"I've taken good care of it."

Indeed he had. But the teacher noted that the edges were much more frayed than his others. Much more "used." As if the pages had been turned again and again over a long period of time.

"I've had it a long time. I just got married last year. And I got a big promotion. I'm a research chemist. I don't think I'll need it any longer. I thought I'd kept it long enough and I knew you'd want it for your shelf. I'm sorry."

The teacher kept turning the book over and over in his hands finding a certain completeness in its familiar feel. Dozens of thoughts raced through his mind, bringing him at last to an understanding of the young man an understanding he'd never found fifteen years earlier.

He slipped the book back into the envelope, fastened the flap, and handed it to the young man. "I'd be honored if you'd keep it."

He took it, but protested, "It would be a shame for you not to have all your books. I know how much they mean to you."

"But I'll always know where it is."

They stopped and shook hands. Their eyes met, and for the first time each one really understood the other.

25
The Baptizing

Everybody in the community had been looking forward to the third Sunday in May at the East Fork Southern Missionary Baptist Church. Of course, the third Sunday of every month was a big day at the East Fork Church because that was "preaching Sunday." The Reverend Sunday James would drive out from Maynardville to do the preaching.

Some said that "Sunday" was a right appropriate name for a preacher. That it was. Some thought he was named for the day of the week, but he wasn't. His mother wanted to have a preacher son, so he was named for evangelist Billy Sunday who she had heard preach once when she was a little girl. The main things Reverend James heard about as a youth were Billy Sunday and how much his mother wanted him to be a preacher like him. And surely enough, with his mother's help, he had felt the "call" when he was ten years old and began preaching in small churches in the area while in his teens. He now served four of these, one Sunday a month at each. His main job was at the chicken plant in Maynardville.

Reverend James would generally arrive about mid-morning. The services would begin with singing by the congregation, after which he would preach for a while. He usually managed to find a stopping place somewhere close to noon. A recess would be called for dinner on the ground prepared by the womenfolk of the church. After dinner, there would be singing by quartets and other groups. Then, Reverend James would preach some more, usually finishing about mid-afternoon. Yes, the third Sunday of the month was always a big day at the East Fork Southern Missionary Baptist Church.

The thing that made May's preaching Sunday so special was the baptizing. Now, a baptizing was not a rare event at the East Fork Church. There would be one every three or four months, and there was sometimes a big one in the summer after the yearly revival meeting. But, the thing that made this one so special was who was going to be baptized.

There were two candidates. Mrs. Pearline Potter was a widow lady who had lived in the community all her life. She had joined the church more than twenty years before, but was not considered a full-fledged member because she had steadfastly refused to be baptized. She had had a bad experience with water as a little girl. One of her brothers had held her underwater down at the swimming hole on Perkins Creek until she almost drowned. From that episode she developed a mortal fear of any water over six inches deep. Even when she bathed, she wouldn't run over three inches of water in the tub. No, Mrs. Potter couldn't be a full member of the church because she hadn't been "put under the waters." She had long felt this separation and knew that many in the church looked down on her.

Reverend James had made her his special project and had enlisted several women of the church to help him show her the necessity of being baptized and to counsel her in this direction. Although it had taken over a year to make any headway, they remained dedicated to their task. Mrs. Potter had finally come around and had agreed to allow Reverend James to "put her under the waters." A big crowd was expected for the event. Some said there might be as many as a hundred people there not counting the children.

Phinos Ledbetter was a different story. He had drifted in five or six years earlier and was just as likely to drift out most any time. He had thrown up a tarpaper shack on the side of one of the hills on land owned by a big coal company that had no immediate use for it. He cut pulp-wood to eke out a marginal living. Phinos spent most week-ends frequenting the local juke joints and drinking and fighting. His weapon of choice was his chain saw, which he always kept in the cab of his pulpwood truck. The roar of his saw had determined the outcome of many fights as it struck fear in hearts of all within earshot. One juke owner had tried to lock him out when he went out to his truck to get the saw, but Phinos cut the door off its hinges and sawed up two tables and several chairs before he ran out of gas.

But Phinos lived in the community and, true to the church's missionary calling, the men of the church tried to bring him to the Lord. For the longest time he resisted all their overtures. Some he ran off with his chain saw when he was in an especially foul mood. But the fall before, Phinos had been the victim of a rather serious accident. It was a Monday and he was pretty well hung-over from the weekend's activities. This condition caused him to get careless, and about half a load of pulpwood rolled off his truck and over him at the same time. Out of it he got a broken arm and ankle and several cracked ribs, plus an assortment of bumps and bruises. During his recuperation, the families of the church took turns bringing him food and taking care of him. They also now had a captive audience for their witnessing and Phinos could hardly afford to turn a deaf ear. When he got back on his feet, he joined the church and quit drinking. Those who weren't interested in Mrs. Potter were surely eager to see Phinos Ledbetter be "put under the waters."

Now, the East Fork Church house was not a particularly imposing structure. It was a small, white, rectangular building with clapboard sides and a tin roof. There was a center aisle with rows of homemade wooden benches on each side. The pulpit stood on a raised platform at the end opposite the door. Heat was supplied by a wood heater which stood in the midst of the benches on the right side about midway of the building. Although rather stark in appearance, the building seemed to fit the setting and the people who attended.

But, there was one unusual aspect of the little church building. It possessed an indoor baptistery. No other country church in the area had one. This was a luxury usually reserved for the more sophisticated town churches and was a source of pride for the members of East Fork.

It was located in an unusual place--underneath the pulpit. The ground dropped off toward the rear of the church leaving several feet between the floor and the ground. This, coupled with the two-foot elevation of the pulpit platform, gave enough room to install a metal tank. The men ran a pipe down from the spring for water and hooked up a small coal stove to heat the water in cold weather. So, the East Fork Church could baptize year-round. They didn't have to wait for warm weather or find a suitable pond or creek. The men built steps inside the tank at one end. Access was gained by moving the pulpit to one side and opening the double doors in the floor. East Fork folks just knew that the other country churches were envious of their modern baptismal facilities.

To give the baptismal candidates a private place to dry off and change clothes, a wire from which a curtain was hung was stretched from wall to wall just behind the opening in the floor. When not in use, the curtain was drawn back to the walls. A second wire ran from the center of the back wall and joined the first wire at its midpoint. Another curtain pulled along this wire, effectively dividing the rear platform space into two areas--one for men, the other for women.

On this particular Sunday, the baptizing was scheduled immediately after the morning preaching and before dinner. Because of this special event, Reverend James found a good stopping place about 11:30 and announced that it was "time for the baptismal waters to be stirred." The curtains were pulled and the two candidates went to their respective areas to wait. Reverend James went with Phinos to get into his waders. The Deacons moved the pulpit and opened the doors. Everything was ready. The house was packed. Folks said there were more than a hundred people there not counting the children, of course.

Reverend James came out from behind the curtain and descended the steps into the baptistery. After reaching the bottom he turned and extended a hand to Phinos, who was dutifully waiting on the platform. The Reverend was one who liked to preach a little over each candidate, and after getting Phinos into position, he began.

"Brothers and sisters, this here's Brother Phinos Ledbetter. He ain't lived long in these parts, but however long it's been, he's been living in sin. He's been bad to drink and cuss and fight and hang out in juke joints. But Brother Ledbetter has seen the light ..." Reverend James paused dramatically with one arm raised—waiting. And he was not disappointed.

From the congregation came shouts of "Praise the Lord!" "Hallelujah!" and "Amen!"

"Brother Ledbetter has done found the Lord!!" Another pause.

Other shouts of affirmation came from all over the building.

"Now, I baptize you, Brother Ledbetter, in the name of the Father, Son, and Holy Ghost." He laid Phinos back and under the water and then up again in a continuous motion. It went off without a hitch.

Phinos sloshed back up the steps and into his area behind the curtain to change out of his wet clothes.

Reverend James called for Mrs. Potter, who came from behind the curtain with some reluctance. Noting this, he came halfway up the steps and offered his hand to reassure and steady her. She set her jaw and resolved to see it through. Her descent was slow as she paused on each step. But, she did get to the bottom and into position.

Reverend James began, "Brothers and sisters, y'all know Sister Pearline."

"SPLOT!" Phinos' shirt hit the hardwood floor.

"Sister Pearline found the Lord many years ago, but she just ain't been complete 'cause she ain't been under the waters."

“SPLOT!” Louder this time as Phinos' pants followed the shirt.

"But today Sister Pearline is gonna be made complete!" Pause.

"Praise the Lord!" "Hallelujah!" "Bless you sister!"

"Now, I baptize you, Sister Pearline, in the name of the Father, Son, and Holy Ghost." As Reverend James began to lay her back, Mrs. Potter's water phobia took control. She screamed and began to kick and thrash about wildly with her arms to keep her head above water. Her hands were searching for anything that she could use to pull herself up. Unfortunately, they found the bottom of the curtain. The sudden strain of Mrs. Potter's pulling caused the wire to snap, destroying all the privacy Phinos had enjoyed a few seconds earlier.

When the curtain fell, Phinos was standing facing the congregation trying to remove his boxer shorts which at that time were in a roll around his knees. A look of terror came over his face as he tried vainly to pull them back up. When the wet fabric did not respond, he jumped straight up and turned to the rear wall, effectively mooning the entire congregation. He was looking for a place to hide or a way to escape, but found neither. There was no rear door, and a glance to either side presented no route of departure. He hopped back around and faced the congregation with his arms crossed over his more private areas.

Reverend James did not realize what was happening with Phinos. He had his hands full with Mrs. Potter, who by this time had dragged a goodly portion of the curtain into the baptistery and was engaged in entangling both herself and Reverend James in its folds.

The instant he got turned back to the front, Phinos spied the only available refuge. He took a couple of shuffling steps and dived head first into the baptistery.

Her struggle with the water was bad enough, but when Mrs. Potter saw a naked man come diving in with her, she went into even wilder hysterics.

Finally, overcoming their shock, several members rushed forward and managed to get a hold on Mrs. Potter and drag her up the steps and onto the platform. However, it was several minutes before she quit screaming and spitting up water.

Phinos wrapped himself in a panel or two of the wet curtains and exited the baptistery without exposing himself any further. Several of the men took him down into the edge of the woods and helped him get dried off and put some dry clothes on. However, they could not persuade him to stay and eat dinner. He said he wasn't about to eat with a bunch of people who'd just been looking at all his private parts.

They let him go on home, but the Deacons thought that somebody from the church should visit him and apologize and try to mend some fences. So a delegation of four or five Deacons tried to do just that the next day. They waited until late in the afternoon after they thought he'd be through cutting pulpwood for the day. However, when they got to Phinos' shack, it was obvious that he'd not worked that day, but had fallen back into the clutches of Demon Rum, or at least one of its close relatives. Probably some moonshine from over in Jakeleg Hollow.

Phinos did not receive them with any warmth. In fact, he

started cussing them as they were getting out of their trucks. He told them that he never wanted to see anyone ever again from the East Fork Southern Missionary Baptist Church, and that if anyone else from the church ever came around him again, he'd take his chain saw and saw the church building down to the ground. They felt sure he meant it, and they beat a hasty retreat when he got his saw out and started gassing it up. The Deacons took Phinos' message back to the rest of the members and nobody from the church ever visited him again.

As for Mrs. Potter, she got a lot of attention during the dinner. The womenfolk were hugging her and telling her how glad they were that she was now a full member. But some dissent arose. Some of the members said that her baptizing didn't count because she'd never been "put under the waters."

Seeing the beginning of disharmony, the Deacons called a meeting right after dinner and went out into the woods to discuss and settle the issue before the afternoon services began. There were Deacons on both sides of the issue but, finally, old Brother Ludlow Sartain cleared his throat and asked for the floor. "Fellows, don't none of us know if all of Sister Pearline ever got under the water all at the same time or not. Only the Lord knows all of what happened in that water this morning. But, I do know this. When she was dragged out, there weren't nothing on her or about her that weren't wet going from the hair on her head down to the tips of her toes. And from as much water as I seen her spit up, I'd say she swallowed enough holy water to baptize a normal size person. So, unless somebody knows for shore, I'd say we don't need to be splitting no hairs with the Lord, and I say we count it."

The rest of the Deacons agreed, and this was announced at the beginning of the afternoon services, accompanied by much shouting and rejoicing.

Later on in the week, several of the Deacons went into Maynardville to inform Reverend James about what had happened with Phinos Ledbetter. They were waiting for him when he finished his shift at the chicken plant. After hearing their report, he kind of walked around in a little circle thinking about what he'd just heard, while absent-mindedly picking chicken feathers off his clothing. Finally he spoke.

"Brothers, we all know that the Lord works in mysterious ways, His wonders to perform. We also know that half a loaf is better than none, and this may mean that one out of two ain't all that bad. So, I say we just rejoice with Sister Pearline and let the Lord see to Brother Ledbetter."

And so they did.

SQUAWK 7500
Terrorist Hijacking of Pacifica 762

Captain Mike Rendell started out his workday like all the workdays before – just another normal day of flying. After spending a raucous night partying with his crew, he and his first officer were looking forward to a nice relaxing flight to the West Coast. "Flaps 1, climb power", Mike repeated as he responded to the command of Gary Ellis, his new-hire First Officer. Mike positioned the flap lever from the "5" spot to the "1" spot and retarded the thrust levers to approximately eighty-eight percent of full power. This was the standard "after take-off" configuration and gave the aircraft its' best rate of climb in relation to burning the least amount of fuel. Pacifica Airlines Flight 762 had just departed from Chicago's Midway Airport. On board the Boeing 737 were 137 passengers, three flight attendants, and two pilots. However, it didn't take long for events to unfold that would thrust Captain Rendell and his crew into one of the most terror-filled days of their commercial airline careers. The lives of his flight attendants and his passengers hung in the balance as Mike battled the elements, a deranged passenger, and aircraft malfunctions as he attempted to bring his fully loaded jumbo jet in for a safe landing.

Author:	**Captain Steve A. Reeves**
Publishing House:	TotalRecall Publications, Inc.
Publication Date:	9/26/2008
ISBN Book:	978-1-59095-844-5
ISBN eBook:	978-1-59095-845-2

Coon Dogs and Outhouses
Volume 2
Short Stories From
The Mississippi Delta

Sometimes I stop and try to figure out where the stories come from and why I write the way I do. I'm sure much of it is a result of the land I grew up on and the people who were trying to scratch a living from it. One of my earliest memories is of a large fire in the middle of the cotton field. It was wintertime and I was helping Daddy burn chunks of stumps and roots which had accumulated during the crop season. It was a new ground farm only recently drained and released from the clutches of the brackish water of a Mississippi bayou. The soil was buckshot - rich, black, and grainy – unlike the light-colored, sandy loam of the old Delta. But the type of soil doesn't matter. If he stays in contact with it long enough, the land will brand a man as surely as the red-hot iron brands a Western calf. I'm sure the flat, almost treeless, bayou studded Delta of my early years which later was replaced by Mississippi's rolling, red-clay hills both placed their marks on me. My family had long been people of the soil and although I chose another profession, I have always been aware of the pull of the land.

Author:	**Luke Boyd**
Publishing House:	TotalRecall Publications, Inc.
Publication Date:	9/26/2008
ISBN Book:	978-1-59095-839-1
ISBN eBook:	978-1-59095-840-7

www.totalrecallpress.com

www.ingramcontent.com/pod-product-compliance
Lightning Source LLC
Chambersburg PA
CBHW070450120726
47910CB00003B/995

* 9 7 8 1 5 9 0 9 5 8 3 7 7 *